COLONIAL RAGNERS

T.N.O.

BOOK 1

JACK MOORE

Chapter 1

The man approaching Danni was relatively short compared to most. The streetlights were bad in this part of town and she could not make out his face but then again, Danni really did not have too. His tan windbreaker, dark pants, and the simple button-up shirt that was only halfway tucked-in were a dead giveaway. So was the man's demeanor. His head was bent slightly forward as he walked through the rain and his body language screamed 'mad at the world!'

Danni only smiled when he got close enough to make out her face. He had a scowl on his and this did not concern her in the least. Norm was almost always doing that. Daniella snickered and told him, "You took your time getting here. I hope you got me some burgers, too."

Norm Scoggins remained serious even if the young girl seemed anything but. He stepped under the overhang to get out of the drizzle and he told her, "I thought about not coming down here at all." At this point Norm gave a close look at what the young girl had on. Her skirt almost deserved the title of belt. Her boots came up over her knees and whatever she had on under her jacket was beyond his description. Norm motioned to her and said, "What's with the get up? Do you think you out here popping johns or something?" Norm rubbed the hair on his chin and then said, "For that matter, aren't you supposed to be back at the station tonight? As I recall you had the duty."

Danni just rolled her eyes, "Oh god, Norm. Now you're starting to sound just like Barbara."

"You know," Norm told her easy enough, "just because Barbara is a pain in the ass most of the time, don't mean she's always wrong." Now Norm gestured to where they were standing, "And whatever we are doing down here, if a Wehrmacht patrol comes by and they happen to see us they might not be too happy about it. This is their turf."

Danni waved it off, "No, it's not. They might have authority over the airport, but this isn't Riggins Field. This is in the city and we have as much jurisdiction here as they do."

That made Norm slide his phone out of his coat and take a look at it. "Speaking of the airport, I have to be there in four hours. I had hoped to get some sleep before then." He looked back at her as he slid the phone back in his jacket,

"And as for the rest of that bullshit, young lady, you damn well know the Germans don't like anybody poking their nose in their business. Every warehouse on this street is contracted out to freight companies. That means the airport, and that means as far as the Germans are concerned, it's their turf."

Suddenly the girl's enthusiasm evaporated as she became much more subdued and even serious, "You know they'll never do anything."

"Whatever it is, Danni," Norm replied right back in a steady and even tone, "they're probably the ones behind it. So, our best play here is for you to go back to the station and do what it is you're supposed to be doing and I go home and get some sleep." As an afterthought, Norm added, "And I'd suggest you put some clothes on while you're at it."

Her enthusiasm came right back, "Look Norm, I made a contact at Feu Rouge tonight. I scored…" He tried to chastise her for even going to that place, but she cut him off before he could get too far along, "No, listen. This guy was sweating buckets. He said something major was moving through the Arch."

Norm just grumbled to himself and rubbed at his chin. He finally decided to ask her, "And did he find you or did you find him?"

Now the young girl back-pedaled, "Well, um…"

Norm sighed in frustration, "You know if they come to you it's always junk. He played you, Danni. Now how much did it cost you? Maybe we can go back down there and wring it out of him."

"No, Norm!" now it was Danni's turn to be frustrated. "You don't get it. He didn't come to me, well not exactly. It was Sally Henchersfield. You remember her? I went to high school with her and…"

"So, Sally calls you at work and you decide to go off to a club and…"

"NO!" Now the girl became downright adamant. "It wasn't anything like that. My CI asked her for help and…"

This story was not getting any better, "Here's another tip, Danni. Anybody that's desperate enough to ask that girl for help don't know enough to be worth wasting your time on. Now if…" The sound of an approaching vehicle stopped Norm in mid thought. Without hesitation he grabbed his young colleague and pulled her into the nearest shadows. He was just sure that a German armored patrol vehicle was going to be turning the corner any second now. He had visions of taking a beating at the hands of heavily armed 'peacekeepers' who would not be too happy about seeing the Colonial Agents poking around their drug business. If Danni's tip turned out to be anything at all that was most likely what it was. Given what Norman knew of that Sally girl, it was better than even money to be the case.

It was something of a surprise to Norman when he saw the vehicle that did appear. It was a truck and not just any truck at that. It was white and had an Interstellar Customs logo displayed prominently on the side. Norm checked the time on his phone again. Danni saw him and knew exactly what he was thinking, "They're closed right now. So, do you believe me?"

Norm made sure their cover in the shadows was good enough. At the same time, he kept his eyes glued on the truck. All the while he asked Danni, "What exactly did this CI say?"

"He said they were moving stuff in and out of this place here," Danni told him as she nodded to the warehouse wall next to them.

"What kind of stuff?"

"He wouldn't tell me everything," Danni replied as she joined Norm in watching the truck park by the loading docks. "He just said if we came down here, we would find out."

Norm groaned as he pulled the pistol out of the small of his back, "This better not be drugs. If it is, I'm going to let the Germans kick your ass."

"I really don't think so, Norm," Danni replied with a somewhat concerned tone. "The guy was scared out of his wits. All he really knew was the stuff they were moving was being kept in these little magnetic cylinders about the size of a large can you'd get at the grocery store."

That drew Norms attention away from the truck, "Magnetic? You mean like industrial storage containers?"

Danni now produced her pistol and a badge. Norm wondered where in the hell she had hid those as he watched her clip the badge to her jacket. As she finished with it, she said, "I have no clue. All I know is what he told me. OK?"

What she was describing sounded like ISCs and Norm knew they had all kinds of uses. Normally what you found in them were things and substances that were not very safe to be in direct contact with. The whole point of the magnetic field generated by the container was to the keep the contents from touching anything else, including the container itself.

There were now several men down on the loading dock. One of them had just driven up with a forklift full of crates. The others were carefully guiding him into the back of the truck. Norm was not really sure what was in the crates, but as his mind chewed on the situation, he was now trying to figure out how he could articulate the idea that he was watching some guys stealing a forklift. It was the middle of the night, all these warehouses were closed, and the light was bad. He couldn't make out the logo on the side of the truck until he had already secured the scene. That would give him the opportunity to see what they were loading up. It would also cover his ass.

"You stay behind me," Norm told his young colleague. Before they walked out of the shadows, he did have one last order, "And if on the off chance we have to pop off do not shoot in the direction of those crates."

Danni gulped, "Um, why?"

In his usual, and somewhat authoritative tone, Norm replied, "If that's what you say it is, the last thing we want are bullets flying around them, clear?"

Danni only nodded before she gulped one last time. She simply followed Norm's lead after that. She kind of wondered if he had a better plan than just walking right up to these guys in the open. If he did then he was not showing it because that was exactly what he was doing. He did hold his pistol behind his back, but past that he showed no other use of any kind of tactics.

When the first of the guys on the platform noticed him, Norm talked in a tone she had rarely heard him use. He sounded happy and pleased! He told the three guys in the jumpsuits, "Guys, have I got a bargain for you tonight! You see this young prime specimen of the female persuasion behind me here? Well some big, strapping, working fellows like you would surely be interested in what she has to offer, I know."

The plan did not go as Norm had envisioned. The three men on the platform had only waited to be joined by their buddy that had been in the back of the truck. They did not even give him a polite brush off. They did not even give him a rude

4

one. Once they were all present, their hands went right for the small sub machineguns that they had strapped to their sides.

Norm's right hand came out from behind him as he jumped for the nearest cover. He got off a few rounds before he hit the concrete and rolled into the nearby wall. He tried to get back up and fire a few more times but he found himself covered in fine concrete dust as the bullets chewed up the top of the small wall. Norm heard some shouts, a truck engine firing up, and the truck pulling away before he could get back up. He knew very little would come of this and he was pissed off enough to run after the truck as it sped off. He hoped he might put a few bullet holes in it before it vanished into the night. When his magazine ran dry he was still not sure if he actually did.

When Norm realized it was over, he found himself standing in the middle of the road with a light rain falling on him while bouncing around like an epileptic. Then Norm yelled out at the memory of the truck, "ASS HOLES!"

He turned and stomped back to Danni. Only then did he see her lying in the parking lot. Norm broke into a sprint and even dropped his weapon without bothering to go back and get it. He landed on his rump next to the young girl. Her stomach looked like it might be ripped to shreds and a stream of blood was trickling out of her mouth. She was still breathing but it seemed to be very painful for her. Danni managed to form one word in a raspy exhale, "Sorry."

Norm pulled her to his lap and began trying to feel past the pool of blood to take measure of her wound. He found himself almost passing out from irregular breathing. The only words he could get out of his own mouth were, "Danni Girl! Don't you do this!"

Norm barely even noticed the bright spotlights on his back or the thick German accent that shouted at him, "Hands out, schnell!"

Chapter 2

The nurses and various emergency room people walked by. They were polite enough but all of them looked at him like he was diseased. They said nothing though. Perhaps they were afraid he would bite. Finally, one of them did approach but even she kept a respectable distance. She tossed Norm a clear plastic bag that had some hospital scrubs neatly folded inside. Norm picked it up off the bench where it landed and then looked at the big white logo on the bag. It was a hazmat bag and he wanted to laugh and cry, "Is that what we are when we bleed out, Patsy? Hazardous Material?"

Patsy was kind of like a clerk in the Emergency room, or at least, that's what Norm thought. She might have been a nurse, maybe even a doctor, but of all the years Norm had been coming in here he had never seen her do more than just make sure all the forms were done right. That did not seem to have really changed because along with the plastic bag she also had her little electronic clipboard.

Patsy remained sympathetic but she also spoke with authority, "You need to get changed, Norm. You're covered in blood for god's sake. If you want to wash all that later, then take it home and do it. But as long as you're in my ER, you're not going to be getting it all over everything, understand?"

Norm never looked up, "I don't suppose I could use the shower while I'm at it?"

"It's an order," Patsy replied. Then she whipped out the clipboard and in a business-like fashion, "Before you do though, is this work related?"

Norm solemnly nodded, "Yeah. You could say that."

"I'll take that as a yes," Patsy replied as she pushed at the screen of her clipboard. "And the patient's full name is Daniella..." Patsy slowed down as she sounded out the words on her screen, "um Patrelli Nu? New? How do you say that?"

Still Norm did not bother to look up. His head was swimming in thoughts. "Nuh-Wen. N-G-U-Y-E-N. Make sure you got it spelled right too." He finally got to his feet, but Norm could not make eye contact with Patsy. He just did not feel like it. As he passed her walking to the showers, he commented, "And just use the station as her address and me as the next of kin."

Patsy did not bother with it. She slid the clipboard back to her side and then looked to Norm who was still walking. Patsy called out to him, "I'm sorry, Norm. I'm sure she'll be ok. Dr. Koch is the best surgeon on the island, if not the whole planet. That's doubly true for this kind of thing."

Norm did not bother to answer her. He walked to the showers and once there he was calling up a phone number even as he pulled off his blood-soaked shirt. It took longer to get an answer than it should have. Norm could guess why. He told the person on the other end, "Tony, get off the damn surfboard and get dressed. You got to be at the airport in a couple of hours."

Tony was not pleased, "I am not on the surfboard, Norm! And why do I have to go to the airport? I thought you were supposed to be doing that?"

"I can hear the waves, Tony," Norm replied as he started working on his pants. "So, if you're not on the surfboard then get your dick out of that girl and do as you're told."

This time it was a female voice that replied, "That's not funny, Norm! We're off work right now and you're the one that Barbara told to pick up the new guy."

Norm took a deep breath and then let his tone bite, "And she's up at Valley. So now I'm telling Tony to do it and I'm telling you to cover for Danni. How do you like that, Amy?"

"Why do I have to cover for her?" Amy groaned.

"Do it and they won't have to pull my foot out of both your asses," Norm growled. They were both complaining as he hung up and threw his phone down on the bench next to the hazmat bag. As he turned and looked at the shower, he wondered if he should have told them what had happened. It took him less than a second to realize he had done the right thing.

On the beach, Tony looked down at his phone and noticed that his background had popped back up and that his phone app had minimized back down in the taskbar. He snickered sarcastically as he looked back to Amy, "Can you believe that guy?"

Amy rolled her eyes and snickered too, "Yeah, does he ever sleep? Speaking of which…"

"Oh, come on," Tony told her. "I don't think we have time to sleep anymore but I can think of one something we do have time for."

Amy pushed him off of her and then started feeling around in the sand for the bottom of her bathing suit. She thought about turning on a flashlight, but they were still within sight of the station and there was the off chance that someone might be prowling around the commissary looking for a soda or late night snack. She complained about that and added, "You know there's nothing wrong with your rack, Tony."

"Why thank you," he replied as he easily found his bathing suit. "I like yours too while we're at it."

She slapped him on the arm, "You know damn well what I mean. For that matter, we could try waiting till we can get back to my place. You know? I did shell out all that money for a crappy little townhouse for a reason." Her hands found her suit and she discovered that it was going to take some serious sand removal before she could even think of putting it back on.

"As I recall," Tony told her as he shook his legs. He was probably doing it for the same reason she was slinging her bathing suit around. He went on, "I didn't have to twist your arm. Besides, I promised you not in the sand and we were not in the sand."

Amy bit back, "Tony, we weren't the only thing all over your surfboard. I got plenty of sand up the crack of my ass, too, thank you very much." Amy stood up off the board and then stomped her foot on it, "And it's as hard a rock. You're not the one with your back on it, you know!"

He slid his arms around her and then kissed her, "I didn't hear you complaining a minute ago."

Amy let him kiss her for a little while and then she broke the embrace. As she began slipping back into her suit, she told him, "I'm serious, Tony. Is this all we have to look forward to for the rest of our lives?"

The look on Tony's face, or at least as much of it as she could make out in the dark, kind of suggested what she had been suspecting. Tony did not know the answer to her question because he had probably never even thought of it. After a moment of silence, he came back with, "Well what do you want me to do about it, Amy? It's not like there's all that much I can."

After Amy finished pulling her top up, she growled at him, "There's plenty you can do, Mister." She stomped off back towards the station house. Tony remained behind, staring into the darkness in disbelief. Finally, he yelled out to her in the distance, "Oh yeah? Like what?"

He could barely hear her yelling back, "You figure it out! Then we'll talk!"

As Amy stepped off the sandy path and onto the concrete porch of the main building, she noticed the lights really were on down in the commissary, and more importantly, she could see the shadow of somebody moving around inside. It seemed that her concerns had not been too far misplaced so she wrapped a towel around her hips and tied it off. She walked a little further than the screen door to listen, but finally just went on inside. She was a little surprised by who she found there. It was not who she had expected.

"Cal," Amy said as she walked into the room, "what are you doing up? I thought Danni had the watch?" Calvin Brandt almost ignored her as he got a can of beer out of the refrigerator and hurried back over to his small computer that he had set up on a messy table. Despite the fact that he was still in his briefs and had on a sloppy looking muscle shirt - in other words having just gotten out of bed - he was also wearing a headset and had a very businesslike look on his face.

Amy put two and two together, "Don't tell me. Norm called and woke you up too?"

Cal held up a finger to signal for silence as he sat down in front of the computer. He was concentrating as he obviously listened to the person on the other end. He then touched the computer screen and called up some files that he quickly sent somewhere else. Amy, being something of a minority on this planet and most definitely the only person that worked here, was actually from Earth. She could never get herself past how archaic the electronics were on this colony. What Calvin was doing right now, and whoever he was doing it with, would have been completely handled by the computer back in the core. Out here they were stuck with crap that was probably two or more centuries behind the times.

When Calvin finished, she asked him, "Are you done yet?"

He finally looked to her and said, "No, they got me on hold."

Yet again, Amy wanted to sneer at how backwards everything here was. She had first moved here when she was in her early teens. Until that time, she had never even heard the term 'being put on hold'. She still thought it was rude.

Amy quickly forgot about that when Calvin finally answered her question.

9

"No, he didn't and I'm going to kill him for it, too." Then Calvin realized and asked, "He called you?"

Suddenly Amy was feeling a sense that not everything was right. She assumed a more defensive posture as she replied, "Not exactly. He called…" Amy then realized what she was saying and changed her story, "Yeah, he called me. He told me to cover Danni on the com-watch. Where is she? Is she upstairs in ops?"

Calvin's face was a bit dumbfounded as he just stared at her. Then he finally told her, "She's in surgery over at Kaiser, Amy. She got shot."

Amy almost fell over. After she recovered from the shock she started thinking. "Was she cleaning her gun or something?"

Cal only grunted at that. Besides, the hospital came back on the line and he had to finish his conversation with Patsy first. In the meantime, Tony came strolling in and went right to the fridge for a beer. As he passed by Amy, she told him the news and he stopped in his tracks. Tony had to think about it for a minute and then he laughed, "You mean she was drinking on duty, right?"

How was Amy supposed to reply to that? Fortunately, she did not have too. Calvin ended his call by thumping the computer screen and then he said, "She asked me to cover for her. She said she had to go take care of something, and well, you know, the only alternative was the Noodle and Poodle show. So, I said what the hell. She wasn't supposed to be gone that long."

Tony was obviously still trying to shift through the information he was getting. He pointed towards the ceiling and said, "Danni's not upstairs?"

Amy just totally ignored Tony, which she did not want to admit but had kind of been the way she was leaning towards as she had left the beach. She announced to her two co-workers, "I'm going back to my old room and change. Then I'm headed to Kaiser."

Calvin did not have any kind of official authority. He was however a generation older than almost everybody that worked here and that usually meant that what he said went despite the lack of any rank. This time was no exception when he said, "No, you're not, Amy. You're going to do exactly what Norm told you to do and man the com-watch. Tony you can help her just in case Barbara calls and I got a feeling she just might."

Tony was still a bit confused, but the one thing he was certainly clear on was, "But Norm told me to head down to Riggins and pick up the new guy."

The reaction was a bit unexpected. Calvin only displayed rightful indignation, "Norm called you, too?" Cal went on further to explain, "I only found out when Patsy just called me for Danni's medical records."

"Too?" Tony was now even more confused and his frustration most definitely showed when he broke out with, "Will somebody explain to me what the hell is going on here?"

Amy just shoved him towards the door that led to the back hallway, "Just do what you're told, Tony. You'll be ok."

At that same moment, a fourteen-year-old in an extra-long night shirt, rubbing her eyes, came stomping in the commissary and headed towards the snack cabinets. She complained the whole way, "You guys are too loud. Do you know that?" A scruffy looking, grayish dog that was part shepherd and part everything else came in right behind her and was sniffing at her heels.

Now Amy almost bit into her, "Shannon, what have we told you about bringing that mutt in…" Amy suddenly caught herself and wanted to bite her own tongue. Then she redirected her anger and frustration at Calvin only she did it in a loud whisper, "I'll take care of this. You just find out what happened!"

Calvin quickly got to his feet and discarded the headset. He talked in a hurried but even tone as he told Amy, "I'm headed over there now."

Tony was still clueless, but he did make an earnest offer to Calvin, "Want me to fly you over there? I thought about taking the bird down to Riggins."

"Hell, no," Calvin said as he grabbed his jacket and only then did he realize he might need some pants. As he headed for his room he continued saying, "There's supposed to be a storm coming so Chuck secured the rotors. He's asleep right now and I barely trust him taking care of that thing when he's wide awake. Do like me and drive down there."

As Calvin vanished into the back hallway, Tony looked to Amy and with no small amount of resolve he said, "So are you going tell me what's going on now?"

Amy glanced toward the young teen and the dog that was still sniffing at her

him on it. At least Frank did the courtesy of moving his shoulders in a slump when he answered, "I told you, man, I haven't seen anybody that fits anything close to what you're talking about. I mean come on, Tippet, you don't even have a picture of the guy. How am I supposed to know who he is?"

Tony just clicked his teeth and turned to walk away, "Keep up the good work, Frank."

Before Tony could get very far, Frank did call out and ask, "Is it true, dude? Did Danni Nguyen really get shot?"

When Tony looked back, he was almost floored by the fact that Frank was no longer leaning on the wall. Maybe the guy had not lost all sense of decency since going to work for the city. Tony walked back to him and remorsefully replied, "Yeah, it's true. She's over at Kaiser Intergalactic right now."

Frank took a deep breath and replied, "Shit." It looked as if he was not too sure what else to say about it. He did manage a couple of completely useless questions though, "Is her Mom still living? I know her old man got killed back when we were still in school. Think I should send flowers or something?"

Tony took it all in and codified his response in a list that he rattled off, "Yes, her Mom's alive but she moved to Teller's Star right after the war. Yes, her Dad got killed and I don't care if you send flowers or not. Maybe chocolate would be better cause I think she has allergies."

Frank seemed to have missed all of that. He just meekly asked, "Is she going to be ok?"

Tony just grumbled, "I don't know, man. Look I got to find this guy asap, ok? See ya." As Tony walked out the front door of the airport he nodded and forced a smile at the Germans who were standing guard there. He got as far away from them as he could without actually having to stand in the rain and then checked his phone. Normally Tony would have been perfectly happy to see that his recent call list was empty. In fact, this was probably the only time he could ever remember that it ticked him off. As he called the first person on his mind, he mumbled, "The one time. Wouldn't that figure."

Cal Brandt answered pretty quickly with, "Have you got him?"

Before Tony answered he asked a question of his own, "Are you there yet?"

"Yeah," Brandt responded. Then he added what he knew was really on Tony's mind, "and the last thing Patsy had for me was that Danni's stable but a long way from being out of the woods. They're still working on her." Now Cal addressed the main reason for the call, "Now what the hell went wrong?"

Tony grumbled in frustration before replying, "It's not my fault, Cal. The guy's just not here. He got off the shuttle. I got that much confirmed but he's not here now."

"You got there late didn't you?" It was all that Cal could think of.

Tony quickly got defensive, "No, I didn't get here late. The guy just isn't here, ok? I waited for him up by the front and he never showed. I know he got as far as check-in, but well," Tony looked back at the Germans and lowered his voice before saying, "but let me tell who is down here. Horst."

"What?" There was no small amount of alarm in Calvin's voice. "What the hell is he doing down there at this time of the morning?" After a moment of thinking Cal said, "That's not our problem. I can't find Norm anywhere."

The one thing that Tony knew about Norm was that he was the guy that you normally did not want to see on your caller ID. For that reason alone, he was usually the guy who was calling. "So, call him."

"I did that, Tony." Cal sarcastically added, "Like I never would of thought of that, you know?" Now Cal became more serious, "I called him, all right. His phone went off, all right. The only problem with that was it was still here at the hospital. It was sitting on the bench in the shower changing room."

The hairs stood up on the back of Tony's neck, "Oh shit."

Chapter 5

The turn off for the L-5 was one of the busier intersections on the entire island. The island was not all that big as far as islands went but if you had to drive from one side to the other you could find yourself missing a couple of hours of your life that might otherwise have been put to more useful endeavors had you bothered to take the controlled access highway. Why it was called the L-5 was not really known by anyone. There was no L-1 to 4 and the letter itself had no known meaning. Somebody had just decided to call it that and the name stuck. Whoever named it, and why, had vanished into history.

The west side exit ramp was graced with a wide assortment of restaurants and shopping plazas that were all competing for the business of rush hour morning commuters. One of the more popular spots was not even noted for its good food. The Foo King Diner had service that was generally less than spectacular, but its cutting edge trumped everything else. It was convenient to get in and out of if you were in a car. That made it quicker to grab a bite before work, even on their slowest of days.

This meant the place was usually packed with a variety of humanity every workday just after the sun came up. This morning was no different. Gracie Palace hated this time of the day for no other reason than by the time it was over her feet hurt. Her job was taking orders, bringing orders and fighting off the advances of more than a few of her customers that wanted to order her just as much as the food.

Gracie walked out to one particular pick-up truck that had pulled into a covered space. She promptly asked the man behind the wheel of the car, "Did you text in an order?"

The guy huffed as he looked out the open window of the driver's side door. He was sweating, his skin looked pale and he did not seem to be in a very pleasant mood. Gracie remembered his vehicle more than his face, but even that looked somewhat familiar. Despite knowing that he was a regular customer, Gracie still wasn't sure exactly who he was. She asked him again and he snapped at her, "NO!" Then after looking at his phone he eased off and said, "Just give me the number one, will you?"

Instead of just walking off with the order, Gracie had to ask, "Are you ok, mister? You don't look too good."

The man did not bother to reply. He was too busy with his phone which he now placed to his ear and scornfully told the person on the other end, "You tell that cock sucker to stay out of our business. I don't care who got shot."

Gracie picked up her step after hearing that and she was still visibly nervous when she reached the order window. She had already sent several orders in via an app on her phone. Now she had to take them back out. Mel, the old scruffy-looking guy that ran the morning window, could not help but notice how jumpy the girl was, "You having problems with your app again, kiddo?"

Gracie tossed a piece of gum in her mouth and began to chew. She nodded towards the pick-up, "That guy out there looks like he's about to fall over in the seat."

"So," replied Mel.

"No, I'm serious, Mel," Gracie shot back. "The guy is as white as a sheet and sweating buckets." She hesitated for a minute and then told Mel the rest, "And he's on the phone telling some guy to shoot somebody."

Mel slid the next set of orders out the window and told the girl, "And exactly what business is that of ours?"

Gracie smacked at her gum, looked at Mel with contempt, and then finally just told him, "Are my orders up?"

Mel vanished into the kitchen, but she could still hear him complaining, "You know Gracie, you're not going to live to be an old woman if you keep worrying about everything. That goes double for stuff that is best left alone. I don't have to tell you that in the Arch, when somebody says they're going to pop a cap in your ass…"

Mel showed back up at the window with the stack of Styrofoam boxes and slid them out to her, "It means they probably are. So those things are best left…"

The heat wave reached them first. Mel's hand went up to protect his eyes from it and then the bright light that came almost immediately after. The sound and concussion waves from the explosion followed quickly on its heels and there was no protection from that. Mel's feet lost their grip on what was, under the best of circumstances, a slippery tile floor. He went down as hard as a rock, and as much as it hurt, he thanked the lucky stars that he was currently seeing in front of his eyes.

Mel had done his time in the war and he knew one or two things about explosions. The best place to be when they happened was as low to the ground as you could get, and preferably with as much solid matter between you and the blast as possible. The concussion wave had worked in his favor this time! What disturbed Mel the most was that, if Mel did not know any better, he would have sworn that the blast had been of the nuclear variety. The only problem with that theory was if it were true then he could not have been making any theories right now. His body would be so much ash floating over air currents well on its way to Valley Point.

When Mel got back to his feet he felt of his forehead and found blood on his fingers when his vision finally cleared up. His kitchen help seemed even more stunned than he was, despite the fact that they had been behind some good cinder block walls that protected them from the worst of it all. It seemed their worst wounds were nothing more than simple shock from the unexpected. Mel cured it with the age-old remedy. He screamed at them in anger, "Don't just stand there, you morons! Get the first aid kit!" The order was quickly tossed around between the help before they finally got to moving.

Mel looked back out his order window and experienced a little shock of his own. The parking lot, specifically the order area, did not look anything like he had remembered. The big awning that sheltered the vehicles when they picked up their orders, was now ripped in half and laying on its side. Several vehicles were on fire and, the most prominent one was the pick-up truck that Gracie had just been talking about. That suddenly reminded Mel of her and he began to panic when he realized he did not see her. Mel did not bother wasting the time to run for the back door when he realized where she was. He just crawled through his window.

Gracie was still intact, more or less. She was laying on the ground next to the window. The blast had thrown her up against the wall but that had not been what killed her. Mel rolled her body over and almost wanted to puke. Only the seasoned mind of a veteran kept his bowels in check. He had not seen anything like this since the war. Half of Gracie looked perfectly normal. Her left side, the side that had faced the blast, was burned beyond all recognition. Mel decided that holding in the contents of his stomach was not such a good thing after all. He let it all come out.

Chapter 6

The clock on the wall was not changing fast enough for Amy. She had left a sobbing fourteen-year-old girl in her room which would have been bad enough under normal circumstances, but Shannon had been doing her best to try and act like a three-year-old after she got the news. Amy had a hard time dealing with the news herself and Shannon's tantrum was not helping. Amy had to wonder if she was supposed to bear the burden for both of them. If it were true, then she knew she could not take it.

That was why Amy wandered upstairs to operations. The place looked as sloppy and run down as the rest of the building, but it had two advantages. One was the row of windows that let you look out on the ocean, and even in the worst of times that had always had a calming effect on Amy. The other was the rows of computers that sat beneath those windows. Right now, any distraction was welcome, and events seemed to be helping out.

Normally, pulling com-watch was a complete and total exercise in boredom. Very little happened at night that would prompt someone to call the Ranger Station. In fact, very little happened in the daytime either. Mostly, the only emergency calls they ever had were from fishermen who got out to sea and had a mechanical breakdown.

A lot of times the boat crews would have the problem fixed before anyone from the station could even get there. Even the ones that did not usually would call a private contractor for a tow before they would let the Rangers do it. No, the only people that really wanted the Colonial Government's assistance these days were those who were too cheap to pay for real help or a few that simply could not afford it.

This morning was proving to be the exception to the rule. Amy was not so sure if this was a good thing or not. She welcomed the distractions, but it was the nature of those distractions that was making her blood pressure go up. She only thought it typical that the biggest crisis they ever had to deal with was their own! By the time anybody else actually bothered to show up for work, Amy was very ready to not only leave. but quit as well.

Shannon had been constantly stomping up the stairs and nagging Amy to take her down to the hospital. Cal had been calling in and nagging about Norm. How was Norm supposed to call in without his phone and wouldn't she call Cal if that happened? Then Tony was calling and sobbing about losing the new boss. He too was hoping for some words that would cure his problem. What was Amy supposed to do about that? This new boss guy had just come from another planet! How was he supposed to call in and say he was lost? The guy probably did not even know how to do it on this world!

When Garcia and Johnson came strolling up the stairs, Amy had never felt more relieved. Then she saw how they were dressed. Her face distorted when she asked them, "Why are you guys wearing ties?"

Garcia promptly flopped down in one of the roller chairs and Johnson went over to the printed logs that he casually began to flip through. It was Garcia who answered, "What? A guy can't dress up every now and then?"

Johnson asked his own question, "The new boss here yet?"

Amy got it real quick like, "You're both a couple of kiss asses, do you know that?"

"Hey," said Garcia taking offense, "I'm not a kiss ass! I just think we should put our best foot forward. Know what I mean?"

Johnson was still busy thumbing through the print- outs. He did not even bother to look at Amy as he raised his hand and in a matter of fact way proclaimed, "He's just trying to look slick. I'm the kiss ass."

The headset that Amy was wearing began to beep before she could say anything else. She looked down at one of the computer screens and gulped when she saw who was beeping her. It was the Colonial Governor's Office. Amy had been half expecting the call. It was about the right time, too. She could see the staff over there wandering in and starting to check their messages. They had probably just finished reading the one about Danni and were now calling to bitch about the impending hospital bill.

Amy practically stabbed the computer screen with her finger as she answered. As if on cue, both Garcia and Johnson began blabbing away with each other as she tried to listen to the person on the other end of the phone. She yelled at them, "Would you please shut the hell up!" Then Amy had to go into damage control, "No, not you! I'm sorry, say that again please?"

Garcia just rolled his eyes at her. Then he swiveled a full three-sixty in the chair before picking up a basketball that had been left by the window some time ago. He started bouncing it on the floor and waited till Amy was off the phone. Then he asked, "What's up with you this morning?"

Johnson finally finished with the print-outs and then casually strolled over to the windows as he asked, "Yeah and for that matter, what are you doing here? I thought you were off today. Didn't Danni have the watch last night?"

"Guys," Amy growled at them, "Danni's been shot. She's in the hospital in surgery! Ok?" Amy began pacing in a circle wondering what to do next. When she saw the file from the Governor's Office pop up on one of the computer screens she wondered what in the hell she was supposed to do with it? Barbara was gone. Norm was missing. Cal was being a dick. And now she was supposed to handle this?

She also ignored Garcia and Johnson who were pounding her with questions about Danni. Amy just raised her hands to her ears and yelled at them. It had little effect. They both only quieted down on their own. At that point Garcia took the floor exclusively and said, "I guess this new dildo American guy we're getting from Earth is going to have his hands full."

Amy only wished the guy was here to have his hands full. Then she finally looked away from the computer screen and saw a strange man standing at the top of the stairs. The guy looked rumpled. His suit was probably expensive, but it looked like it had been through the mill. He also had a thick layer of mud on his pants and shoes. Some of it had splattered all the way up one side of his coat.

Amy was a bit startled to begin with, but she quickly forced a recovery and said, "Can I help you with something?"

The guy came strolling in without answering her question. His shoulders were square, and he walked in a particularly upright fashion. His eyes were narrow as he seemed to take in and memorize every little detail in the room. Garcia stood up and in a forceful way he demanded, "Hey, buddy. Who the hell do you think you are?"

The man looked over his shoulder with a side glance and replied to Garcia, "I'm the dildo American guy."

Garcia gulped. Johnson slumped and just mumbled towards Garcia, "Way to go, hot shot."

The guy squared off with Amy who was starting to look like she wanted to crawl right out a window. He then said, "You look like you might actually know what's going on around here. I'm Deputy U.S. Marshall Jacob Barton."

Amy adjusted her shoulders and then quivered before saying, "I'm Agent Amy Hiller. I was just... well, um... we sent somebody to pick you up!"

Barton began to slip off his jacket and Johnson quickly ran over to take it but Barton would not let him. Barton then commented, "That's a hell of a driveway you guys got coming down here."

Garcia gulped again and then noted, "You must have tried to drive thru that big puddle. You kind of got to go around it."

Barton ignored him and tossed his dirty jacket over the back of an unused chair that was already filled with junk. Then he began to work at the buttons on the cuff of his shirt as he asked Amy, "I just came over here from the US Consulate. I was having breakfast with this Whitman guy; you know the head cheese over there. He got some kind of note and the only good thing I can say about that is it interrupted a rather pathetic breakfast that included eggs that tasted something like cardboard. He also wouldn't bother to tell me what the note was about but said somebody over here would."

Amy shivered and just said, "I have no idea?"

Jake finished rolling up his sleeves before stating, "Well it must be something important cause it ended our meeting. Anything big happen around here this morning?"

Garcia mumbled, "That would be an understatement."

Amy thought she was about to puke. Then she saw the next person walking up the stairs and she could not remember a time when she was ever so glad to see Norm. As he got into the room, he took one second to notice Garcia and Johnson. In a semi angry way, he rhetorically asked, "What you two supposed to be? Clowns?" He then walked right past the new boss and Amy before he began calling up files on the computer.

Amy quickly cleared her throat and said to him, "Uh, Norm, this here is Deputy Barton, you know, our new boss."

Norm never looked up from the screen. He did manage to raise one hand, in a wave, as an afterthought, "How you doing, Barton. Be with you in one second." As he kept right on looking for files he did manage to say to Amy, "I lost my phone, Amy, I need somebody to burn me another one real quick."

Amy meekly and nervously answered, "Cal has it. You left it at the hospital."

Whatever Norm had been looking at he quickly closed and then he finally made eye contact with Amy, "Call him and tell him to get back over here. I'm probably going to need him."

"Um," Amy just tugged at his sleeve and pointed back to the new arrival, "Boss...New...Here...Now."

"I got that from the top, Amy," he told her as if it were of no consequence to him. Then Norm looked at the guy.

It was Jake who spoke first, "So are you the guy in charge? Funny, you don't look like a Barbara."

Norm laughed that off in a way that made it clear that his humor was both disingenuous and annoyed. He told the guy, "She's not here right now. She's up at our station at Valley. I kind of run things when she's not around."

Garcia mumbled, "And when she is, too." Norm looked to Johnson who promptly slapped Garcia in the back of the head.

Norm went on after that, "I'm Agent Scoggins and you'll have to forgive us. We had an officer down last night. It's had things in kind of an uproar around here."

Jake just looked at all of the faces around him and then asked Norm, "So is that the big emergency that has the US Console in an uproar?"

Norm just shrugged, "Maybe. I kind of doubt it though, and to be honest with you, Deputy, I really don't give a shit what has Whitman's panties in a wad. He's not the most popular person around these parts."

Amy began tugging at Norm's sleeve again and pointing to the little file icon on one of her computer screens, "We just got that from the Governor's Office!"

Without ever breaking eye contact with the new boss, Norm asked Amy, "Is it about the hospital bill?"

Amy quickly replied, "No."

Norm made his decisions without even thinking, "Then send Tony."

27

"Um," Amy gulped again. "He's not here. He's out," she gestured to Jake and continued, "looking for him."

Norm then answered without so much as a blink, "Where's Cal right now? Send him."

"Um," Amy was getting even more nervous and meek. "I don't know. He's out, um, kind of looking for you."

Jake broke into the conversation with a very authoritative, but somewhat sympathetic sounding question, "What's the governor want, Agent Hiller?"

Amy let out the breath she had been holding in, "There was an explosion over at the west end of the L-5 just a little while ago."

Now Norm sounded agitated and he looked at Amy, "That's the fire departments job. Why are they calling us about it?"

"It's not a rescue mission, Norm," Amy finally bit back. "Some people were killed and they want us to look into it."

Now it was Jake's turn. When Norm locked eyes with him again, Jake broke into a bemused smile and told him, "Sounds important, Agent Scoggins. Since you don't seem to know where any of your people are maybe you and I can go out and have a look?"

Rising to the challenge, Norm replied, "Yeah, maybe we should, Deputy Barton."

After the two men vanished down the staircase, Johnson called after them with just enough volume not to be heard, "You know some of us are sitting right here!"

Now Amy went from meek to commanding as she began to walk out, "Which is exactly where you're going to stay, Bob. I have to take Shannon over to the hospital."

As Amy descended the stairs Garcia got up and ran after her, yelling back over his shoulder, "Sorry, bro, but you just got tagged it!" He was gone before Johnson could even protest

Chapter 7

The uniformed officer at the perimeter did not seem to be of the opinion that they should be allowed on the crime scene. Norm even pulled out his badge and showed it to the guy. The officer was not very impressed. He simply said, "I got orders not to let anybody in." Norm pulled his badge back in the car and dipped his head as he mumbled something. Jake thought that it sounded like the man was angry at summer. It made no sense, so Jake let it pass.

What Jake did in response was to get out of the passenger side and then he walked around the car. He squared off with the officer who proved to be every bit Jake's size. Norm watched as Jake whispered something to the man. When Jake got back in the car he said, "Drive on, Agent Scoggins." Sure enough, the officer got out of the way.

When Norm parked the car just beyond the host of fire trucks, he had to ask the American, "What did you just tell that guy?"

"You don't want to know," Jake said with a straight face. He got out of the car after that and Norm decided he had better do it too. As both men walked past the firetrucks, they surveyed the burned-out vehicles, the damaged building, and the marks on the pavement where bodies had been laying. Ambulances were still treating casualties and firemen were still poking around looking for whatever. When Jake commented he said it all, "I've seen some war zones that look better than this."

Norm just nodded and looked for the main man he figured he would need to talk with. Instead, he found the chief of the local police. Norm would have avoided the guy completely, but he came to Norm and said, "I heard Nguyen got shot last night."

Norm nodded in the affirmative and replied, "Yeah, Hal, and I heard you didn't go see her."

If the man took offense, he didn't show it. He just replied, "Word is that she was with you when it happened."

Norm just responded by asking, "Is there something you want, Hal?"

The Chief of Police pointed to Jake, "Who's your friend here, Norm?"

"I can introduce myself," Jake let everybody know before he told the man who he was. Jake did not bother to shake hands.

Then Norm came back with, "Um, this here is the local chief of police, Hal Summers." Norm had to add, "And he's the wrong chief. I need to talk with Tippet."

"Wasting your time here, Norm," Hal replied. He turned and walked off. As he did, he called back, "Nothing here to see."

Now Jake fully understood what Norm was talking about back in the car. He let it go and asked, "Who's Tippet?"

"Fire chief," Norm replied just as he spotted the man. As they walked to him Norm explained, "You haven't met Tony yet. This guy is his uncle." Norm stopped just short of the fireman and let the guy finish talking with some of his captains. When Tippet finished, he walked over and shook hands with Norm. Jake noticed that the fireman's smile looked genuine enough, which had most definitely not been the case with the cop. Norm finally got around to asking, "So, what happened here, Blake?"

"Near as we can tell," Blake pointed one of his burly fingers at what was now little more than a charred frame. Jake could guess that it had been some sort of automobile. The fireman went on, "That's where the explosion was centered."

Jake introduced himself and then asked, "Hydrogen cell?"

That took the fireman by surprise. He shook it off and then answered with a simple and confused, "Um, no."

Norm cut in with, "You'll have to forgive Deputy Barton here. He just made planet fall a few hours ago."

The fireman almost laughed and then told Jake, "Well, I guess they popped your cherry real quick, didn't they, pal. No, we don't use hydrogen here."

Norm pointed across the L-5 at a fueling station and in particular at its sign.

Jake almost chuckled, "Benthic Petroleum? I didn't even know those guys were still in business."

"They are out here in the colonies," Norm told him. "This planet has a pretty good-sized crude reserve so it's cheaper just to burn gas."

Blake Tippet crossed his arms and added, "Yeah, well, that was no gas tank that went up. Hell, I'm not even sure what it was. I just know that there isn't anything on a vehicle that could cause this. My guys have found debris over a mile from here."

Jake asked, "So, what you're saying here is this was a deliberate explosion? Some kind of car bombing?" Jake looked up at the sign for the restaurant and then said, "So, who would want to blow up the Foo King Diner?" He suddenly realized what he said, "Well, that guy had a sense of humor."

Norm replied, "No, that's his real name."

Jake nodded and came back with, "Ok, so his parents had a sense of humor. So, who'd want to blow this place up?"

"Nobody." Norm replied off the cuff before asking the Chief, "Is it safe to go over there now?"

Blake laughed before getting back to work, "Safer than it was just before the explosion."

Norm wandered over to the edge of the black marks that were nearest to the vehicle that had been at the epicenter. He just stood there silently and looked. Without even noticing if the new boss had followed him, Norm asked, "You're supposed to be some kind of super soldier. What do you make of this?"

Jake crossed his arms and said, "I can't say for sure what did make it, but I can tell you what didn't."

Norm looked back at the guy and said, "I'm listening."

Jake squatted down and pinched some of the scarred asphalt. He rubbed it between his fingers and then made a little circle with a single finger in the ash. When the Deputy Marshal stood back up, he pointed to the frame of the truck and said, "What's missing?"

Norm also had his arms crossed but struck a more thoughtful pose as he asked, "That was all just bullshit you were doing down there in the dirt, right?"

"The crater," Jake told him. "An explosion this big should have left a crater. They should have had to dig that frame up out of the mud about twenty feet down."

"So, what's that supposed to mean exactly?" Norm asked.

"What it means, Agent," Jake replied as he rolled up his sleeves, "is that whatever did this wasn't a conventional explosive. Any chemical explosives that could throw debris over a mile away would have put a fair-sized hole in this parking lot. You got a knife?"

Norm was a little surprised by the question and he replied with, "I'm surprised you don't have a big one with a compass in the hilt."

"Cut me some slack," Jake told him. "I just got out of airport security. You think they're going to let me pass with a blade?"

Norm reached into his pocket and tossed the man a pocketknife even if he was not entirely sure what the guy wanted to do with it. As Jake unfolded it, he then began looking around. As for exactly what he was looking for, well, Norm had no clue. As Jake looked some more he explained, "That was a high energy burst, whatever it was. It was enough to melt the asphalt under the ash. All the way out to here too."

Jake's eyes locked in on a man who was standing over by the diner's service window. The guy was passionately talking to a couple of firemen. Norm followed the deputy over and listened to him ask for some vinegar. The diner guy seemed more than happy to provide it, so while Jake was on a roll he also asked for some wax paper and a writing instrument too. The man had both and produced them in short order.

Norm commented as he watched the goods change hands, "Good thing somebody didn't try and blow up an accounting office or you'd have never found a pencil."

Jake just gave the man a sly look and walked on out to the frame where he proceeded to get his clothing completely dirty as he got down and started looking around the frame. Norm watched from a safe distance and asked the guy that had gathered the supplies, "You work here I take it?"

"Yeah, I run this window right here," Mel told the guy. Then he looked over the scrubs the man was wearing and asked, "Are you a paramedic or something?"

"Colonial Ranger," Norm replied as he closely watched Jake doing whatever he was doing. Norm did ask the cook, "Were you here when it went off?"

"Yeah," Mel thumbed to the window, "was right in there. I tell you I done me a war and I would have swore that blast was a nuke."

Norm crossed his arms again and was still intently watching Jake. The guy had poured the bottle of vinegar on a part of the frame and was now scratching at it with the pocketknife. Norm still managed to ask Mel, "Why do you say that?"

"The heat, the light, then the blast itself," Mel told the guy. Then he pointed at the wall behind them, "Hell, look at what it did to my wall. This used to be light blue." Mel was getting the impression he was only being half listened to so now he asked a question of his own, "What's your buddy doing out there?"

"I think I just figured it out," Norm said as he walked off. He stopped over Jake and asked, "So, did you find the VIN number?"

Jake stood up with the wax paper in his hand and pointed to the rubbing he had just made, "Not all of it, but it's enough I hope."

After being handed the paper, Norm looked at what they had and said, "Eight characters. They're usually fourteen. It should narrow it down and then all we have to do is cross reference that with any missing persons that show up in the next couple of days."

As the two men walked back to Norm's car, they ran into a very impatient looking Calvin who promptly tossed Norm his phone. As he did Cal also added, "Darcy has called three times already. Where the hell were you?"

Norm answered by pointing to Jake, "This is the new boss. New boss, this here is Cal Brandt." Then Norm had his own question, "Since you found us, I'm guessing you already talked to Amy?"

"Yeah, I did," Cal replied. "Speaking of finding things. You didn't have your

33

phone, Norm. How did you find this place? Amy never told you where it was."

Norm walked on past the man as he replied, "I looked for the firetrucks. How else do you find a fire?"

Chapter 8

It was the sudden and repeated stabs that finally got Amy's attention. The biggest thing about them were how much they hurt. Her eyes flew open and she grabbed for her arm as she proclaimed, "Ow!" Then she suddenly realized how much her neck hurt as well. She was busy massaging it when she suddenly realized that she had no idea where she was. There were plain walls, uncomfortable seats, and there was a computer screen stuck up on the wall that was running all news bulletins. There was also a fourteen-year-old girl sitting next to her with unusually long fingernails. That explained the stabbing.

Amy yawned and rubbed her eyes as she asked, "Did we get any word?"

Shannon used one of her nails to point up at the door to the hospital waiting room. Amy followed the line and found herself looking at some dark headed woman dressed in expensive clothes. The woman took her sunglasses off and Amy felt a spark of recognition there but could not quite put a name with the face. Maybe it was the lack of any descent sleep, or quite possibly, Amy never really knew the woman's name in the first place?

"Do I know you?"

The woman had a slight accent when she spoke, "Yes, you should. You are Agent Hiller, right?"

The slight accent gave the woman away. Amy had heard it many times since she moved to this planet and it gave her a little direction about what to do. She sent Shannon down to the snack machines and then stood up to face the woman, "Tasha Kingsley, right? Is there something you want?"

The woman seemed a bit peeved when she replied to Amy, "Well, of course I do. A friend of mine has been shot. I would like to know how she is doing."

"Excuse me?" Amy replied with a little bit of confusion, "Your friend?"

"Daniella is my friend," replied the Kingsley woman. "We went to school together."

Amy was not really sure what to say. She fidgeted and it did not take long before this Tasha woman told her, "I know she probably has not spoken of me Agent Hiller. Probably for the same reason you are giving me that look right now."

"What look?" Amy scrambled to try to cover herself, "I don't have a look! I'm just, uh, well I didn't get a lot sleep last night as you can image I…"

"Do not lie," Tasha told Amy. "I have been married to that bastard for six years. I know that look when I see it. Well, agent, I am not my husband and Danni is still my friend. I want to make sure she is all right and I want to see if there is anything I can do."

"Oh," Amy just fidgeted some more. She tried to think of something to say but, finally decided to just ask, "So, I guess you haven't seen her lately, have you? She's doing fine…" Amy suddenly realized what she had just said and corrected herself, "I mean she was before she was shot and all. Um, so how have you been?"

Tasha only groaned in frustration and said, "I knew this was a mistake. Still I had to come because I love Danni so. Even when that angry little policeman so much as accused me of shooting her, I still come. Is that not enough for you cops?"

Amy squeaked, "I guess?"

Tasha rolled her eyes just before reaching in her purse. Amy had visions of a gun coming out and shooting her right between the eyes. Fortunately, all the woman pulled out was a small business card that she offered to Amy. Then the woman said, "That's my private number. Just scan it if she needs anything. I know she has no more family here, so I am here for her."

Shannon came back with far more snacks than she probably should have had. Amy did not complain in the least because for some reason Tasha Kingsley turned around and walked out no sooner than she saw the teenager. Amy deflated even if Shannon did not seem to notice. The kid just tossed her thumb towards the hall and said, "That doctor is out there now."

"Shit," Amy rushed pass the kid and practically ran down to the nurses' station. Sure enough, the German doctor was standing there talking to a nurse. When Amy asked him the question all she got was a shrug from the man. It was the nurse who told Amy, "He doesn't speak English, dear."

Amy frantically asked the nurse, "You were talking to him?"

Maybe the nurse was being a smartass when she replied with a, "Jahol, herr frau."

"Translate," Amy snapped back. "Is she going to live?" The nurse was still amused as she asked the doctor in German. Once again, the doctor only shrugged. Amy grunted as the nurse went on to say, "Your friend is out of surgery. They moved her to Intensive Care. There's no way to tell at this point, darling. I'm sorry. I wish we could tell you better news but with these things we just don't know."

"Can we talk to her?" Amy asked. It was like grasping at straws, but she felt like doing it right now.

"She's not conscious," the nurse replied. "Why don't you go get some sleep. You look like you could use it. We'll ring if something changes."

Amy did not do as told. She stumbled back to the waiting room and found that they now had additional company. Tony was sitting beside Shannon and they were passing a handheld game console back and forth between each other. They seemed to be having a good time which was contrary to the way Amy was currently feeling.

When Tony looked up and saw Amy at the door he asked, "What happened? Is she ok?"

"ICU," Amy glumly replied as she found her another seat to occupy. She buried her face in her palms and then the rest of her head vanished beneath her long red hair. Then, with no small amount of frustration, she jerked up and growled, "Oh this day is just turning out to be grand!"

Shannon paused her game and asked, "Who was that woman?"

Tony quickly perked up at that, "What woman?"

Amy forced a fake smile, "Oh, Danni just got paid a goodwill visit by the

Texian Legion."

"Excuse me?" Tony replied.

"As it turns out," Amy tried to figure out how to explain it. She couldn't figure out any delicate way to say it, so she went with, "Her and Tasha Kingsley were BFFs in high school apparently."

Now Tony was even more confused, "Wait a minute. I knew Danni in high school, well she was in eighth grade when I was a senior."

Amy began rubbing her forehead, "Was that before or after they held you back?"

If Tony took it as an insult, he did not show it when he said, "After." It came out in a very matter of fact kind of way. He also sounded distracted until his eyes lit up and said, "Holy shit. She used to hang out with this girl named Natasha, um, Ivanov. Oh my god, that girl is Tasha Kingsley?"

Now Amy stopped rubbing her forehead and slapped it instead, "How could you not know that, Tony? My god, that woman is on the cover of every fashion magazine in the Arch."

"Well first off," he replied as he ticked off points on his fingers, "I haven't looked at a fashion magazine since I was twelve and…" Tony's eyes drifted down to Shannon and so he revised his statement, "I never seen one. Second, if that's her then she's changed a little bit since junior high. The girl I knew was buck tooth and flat chested."

Amy shook her head in disbelief, "Tony, every girl is flat chested and buck toothed in junior high."

Shannon snarled, "Watch it, sister!"

"I'm sorry Shannon," Amy apologized in a less than convincing manner. Then she turned her attention back on Tony, "You know she is married to the son of the kingpin, and heir apparent, of the Texas Mob. I'd bet she could afford braces at some point. I'm willing to bet those…" now it was Amy's turn to look over at Shannon and figure out what to say next.

Shannon saved her the trouble, "Oh, they were definitely not real."

37

Now Tony was sitting up with his back noticeably stiff and he traded glances with Amy. Then he asked her, "Did Norm say what they were doing last night?"

"No," Amy replied, "Cal told me that Danni got a call and had to go take care of some business. Norm never told me anything. Hell, he was running around all morning without his phone."

"Yeah, I know," Tony told her with no small amount of frustration in his voice, "I tried calling him. Did he ever show up?"

"Yeah," Amy nodded deep in thought. "He and the new guy went to some fire over by the L-5." She could see the confused look forming again and Amy put her hand up, "Don't ask, it's stupid." Then she got back on her train of thought, "He should have his phone by now. I told Cal where to find him. Hell, I couldn't even send Norm the file on the case because he…"

As Amy drifted into deep thought and silence, Tony had to reach over and poke her to get her back to reality. Then Amy asked in a very quizzical way, "How did he know where to go? I never told him where it was?"

Tony reached into his pocket, pulled out his phone, and hit the button for Norm. After a few minutes he hung up and groaned, "Oh great, he's still not answering."

That set Amy into motion. She produced her phone, but she called Cal, "Where are you? Are you guys still at the crime scene, err, whatever it is?"

Cal seemed a little surprised when he answered, "No. I brought the new boss back to the station. Why? What's up?"

Amy put her hand over the microphone and in a hushed tone she told Tony, "Cal's back at the station." Then she tried to pretend everything was all right as she asked, "Is Norm there by any chance? I guess you didn't get him his phone, did you?"

"Yes and no." Cal corrected himself, "Well more like no and yes, I mean. No, Norm isn't here and, yes, he has his phone. He's not there with you? He should be there already."

Amy did her 'everything is all right' voice, "I'm sure he's just caught in traffic. Talk to you later, Cal!" She hung up before Cal could say anything else. Then she got dead serious, "Cal has no idea where he is."

Chapter 9

The shower stopped running in record time. Darcy looked away from her computer screen and lifted up her glasses so she could read the time on the wall clock. He was usually in the shower twice as long, but somehow this did not surprise her. When Norm had come stomping in the kitchen door he looked as if he was of a single-minded determination, the likes of which she had not seen in a long time. The man barely even noticed her and pretty much brushed her off while on his way to the bathroom.

Somehow, the only real answer he gave her did not help matters any. When Darcy questioned him about why he was wearing hospital scrubs, and consequently what had happened to the clothes he left the house in, all Norm had said was, "They had blood all over them, baby."

Norm came strolling out of the bathroom still partially wet and wrapped in a towel. Darcy pointed over to the bed where his phone lay on top of the scrubs he had discarded, "Somebody called you."

"I don't want to talk to nobody right now," was all he said as he began rummaging through his drawers.

Darcy turned around in her desk chair, let her glasses fall to the end of their chain, and got stern, "Why is it you're trying to act like I'm not even here, Norm?"

At least this time he partially looked back before he went about his business, "I wasn't expecting you to even be home right now."

Why was it that this did not make Darcy feel any better, "It's a teacher work day. I decided to log in from home and grade papers here. I did that mainly because I thought you'd be home early."

Now Norm was at his closet looking for pants. He gave a quick turn to his wife and smiled at her, "And so I am."

"Yeah, Norman," Darcy did not return the smile, "but you're running right back out. You're running around here like you're a cop all over again. You promised me when you left the department that all of that was behind you." This time he did not bother to answer her. He was definitely moving to only one tune this morning.

Darcy crossed her arms and huffed. Then she asked, "Who called you last night?"

He was almost mumbling as he slipped into a shirt, "I told you that last night. It was Danni."

"And where is she right now, Norm?" Darcy stood up after that question and then asked her original question one more time, with a qualification, "And who really called you last night? I can't remember the last time anybody from that fucked-up little office ever called here and drug you out in the middle of the night. Even Barbara has got more sense than that."

When Norm did not reply, Darcy went on, "Why don't I just call Danni right now and ask her?"

Norm slipped his jacket back on, put his phone in his pocket, and then his gun in the small of his back. He walked by his wife, gave her a quick kiss, and then went back to his chest of drawers. He took two extra magazines of ammunition out from under some socks and slipped them into his jacket pocket.

Finally, he told his wife, "You can't do that, Darcy."

With her hands on her hips she replied, "And why can't I?"

Norm gave his wife one more kiss. She was just as non-responsive this time as she was the first. Then he told her, "Cause she's in surgery right now, Darcy. She took two bullets, one in the chest and one in the abdomen."

Darcy felt her stomach turn. She fell to a sitting position on the bed and gulped. She knew Norm was not kidding. He seldom joked about anything and would never do so about something like that. Darcy huffed out a few words, "Is she going to be all right?"

"I don't know, babe," said Norm as he walked to the bedroom door, obviously on his way out.

Darcy called out to him, "Where are you going, Norm?"

He did stop this time. Norm sniffled and rubbed at the hair on his chin as he thought about what to say. Then he told her in no uncertain terms, "You know you can't ask me that. It's better if you don't."

Now Darcy was back on her feet. She wanted to grab him, stop him, as he was on his way to the door. Darcy chased after him and when Norm tried to go out the kitchen door, Darcy put her hand on it and stopped him, "Why, Norm? Why?"

Norm licked his lips and then looked at his wife. He was trying to be patient. She could see that in her husband. but as in the past, it was a losing battle. Yet he was calm when he told her, "Danni got herself into something. Whatever it was, it involved some dangerous people, Darcy."

Darcy got in his face and made him make eye contact with her, "This is about revenge, isn't it? This is about that little girl's father, isn't it? That wasn't your fault, Norm."

This time, Norm did blow up, "I know that!" He backed off and composed himself before trying to explain, "Look, Darcy. I can't tell you what I got to do right now, but you're just going to have to trust me. I have to do this."

This time he did walk out. This time Darcy let him go. This time she did not want him to see her cry.

Chapter 10

The first reaction that Jake had when he opened the door was to cough. As he furiously fanned the air with a squinted face he had to ask, "What died in there?"

Bob Johnson pushed his way past his new boss and rushed into the room with a single-minded determination. He ran right for the window cranks and began to let some fresh air into the corner office. After he got both sets of windows cracked, he discovered the slight breeze was disturbing the dust that had settled on the boxes and tarps that were scattered around the room.

41

Jake built up his courage and stepped into the room. His second reaction was, "I thought you said there was already a desk in here?"

"Um," Bob started peeping under tarps and when he got a smile on his face, he pulled back the canvas he was peeping under. It set off a small avalanche of junk but did indeed display a desktop.

Jake pointed at the smudge on that desktop, "What the hell is that?"

"It's your desk," Bob replied with a smile. Then he saw what Jake was really pointing at. There were some splattered remains of local wildlife smeared across the top. What was left of the animal's body was now deposited in two separate locations. Even Bob had to step back and pinch off his nose. He did comment, "I hope I didn't do that."

"From the looks of those wounds, Agent," Jake told him, "I'm kind of hoping you did. Otherwise I'd hate to meet the thing that ripped that in two. What is that anyway? A miniaturized tank?"

Bob was now frantically looking around the room for a broom and dustpan. He was sure that they had left them up here last year sometime. As he did, he explained, "A lot of the local sea life here has that scaled type of defense. Don't worry though, they're mostly harmless. They don't like the way we taste."

Jake just waved off his agent and decided to give up on seeing his new office. It was on the second floor of the building and at the end of a long hall that came out of the ops center. As near as Jake could tell not a single room up here, save the actual ops center, had been used in years. Apparently, Jake's new command was really good in the field because it was clear that they didn't ever do anything in an office.

"This is way beyond the capabilities of your average dustpan, Agent," Jake told him. Jake also made sure the door was closed when they were both out of the room. Then he asked the agent with the tie, "Where does this Barbara person do her work?"

"Oh," Johnson developed a smile. From the look on his face he obviously had expected a much harder question, "Well she has a little workstation set up down in the room that her and her daughter live in."

Jake pointed down at the floor, "She actually lives here with a kid? On purpose?" Jake did not wait for an answer. He started walking back towards Ops. It might not be tidy but at least it was relatively clean. As he walked back down the hall, with Johnson in tow, he had to ask, "So, do all you guys live here?"

"Oh, hell no!" Johnson said with a matter of pride. Jake took that to mean he didn't live here. Johnson confirmed it as he explained, "Just Barbara and her daughter, Shannon, along with Cal, Danni, and... Oh! Yeah, I guess I should count Chuck."

"Who's Chuck?" Jake asked as he finally made it back into the ops center.

"He's our mechanic," Bob explained. "He keeps the helicopters flying and the boats from sinking. Only he lives out at the hanger. He doesn't come down here too much. I don't think him and Barbara... Well it's complicated."

Under his breath, Jake mumbled, "Big fucking surprise there."

It did not seem as if Johnson noticed the mumbling, "And of course there's Tony."

"Tippet," Jake added as he turned the corner rail to walk down the staircase.

Johnson hung right on his heels, "Yeah. He doesn't actually live here, well not most of the time anyway. He hangs out here enough he might as well." Almost as an afterthought Bob added, "We got plenty of room if you need a place."

"Thanks," Jake said as he walked in the commissary, "I'll get a hotel room." Jake stopped behind Calvin who was sitting next to his little computer workstation. Jake asked him, "Find anything?"

Cal thumped his computer screen and the printer next to it began to whirl to life. Jake could not help but think about the last time he heard a printer make that kind of sound. Then he realized it was never. Cal pulled the paper out of the chute and summed it up for Jake as he read, "Just got that file in from KKH Motors. That's the number of possible Vehicle Identification Numbers that could fit what you had."

Jake pointed to the paper, "This is good news. There's only like twenty registrations on here."

"Twenty-three actually and, yeah, that much is the good news," Cal said with a certain tone in his voice that spelled out there was a downside to this. "Turns out, that kind of VIN is only for pickup trucks and they only have ten characters instead of fourteen. Those are also all older models. The new ones have a hell of a lot more."

"So," Jake shrugged, "what's the catch?"

"Well they don't have a clue who owns them," Cal said. The dumbfounded look from the new boss told Cal he had best explain, "KKH just makes 'em. They don't sell 'em."

That did nothing to dispel the dumfounded look. Jake huffed and said, "You people don't have something like a DMV on this rock? How do you collect taxes if you don't know who owns what?"

Johnson pointed at the paper and said, "Yeah we do, but they track plates and not VIN numbers."

Now Jake growled, "That's got to be the stupidest thing I ever heard. What if…"

Cal nodded and broke in with, "Yeah, the auto theft lobby has quite some influence here."

"OK," Jake waved his hands around and decided to pursue another angle. "The dealers have to track this stuff. Why don't we call them?"

Cal just shrugged, "I'll give it a try, but remember, older models. We don't even know if the lot that sold it is in business anymore."

Johnson perked up, "Might as well start with the big ones. They've been in business the longest. There's only three or four of them on the whole island."

Once again, Jake saw a downside despite the fact that Johnson sounded optimistic. Maybe that was the problem? He sounded just a little too much so. Jake asked, "And how many small dealers?"

Cal did not sound as enthused as Johnson when he said, "Close to fifty, probably."

Well that made it clear, at least to Jake it did. He handed the paper back to Cal and said, "Well, get everybody in here and let's start calling."

Cal dropped the paper on his small desk and then he diplomatically brought up a point by first asking if he could. When he got the go ahead, he said, "Remember, we're not just calling all these dealers. We're asking them to run over twenty something numbers, too."

"So?" Jake replied.

"Well," Cal tried being even more diplomatic, "you know they do have other things to do like, um, selling cars maybe? Some of them might not want to cooperate, and even the ones that do… well, we don't know if we can even trust their records."

Jake was not sure he got the point here. He looked dumbstruck once more and then asked, "How hard can it be to run a few numbers on a computer?"

It was Johnson who pointed out when it finally occurred to him, "Yeah, that would be assuming that they even have that. A lot of small businesses here don't use computers. You know we don't have anything like an internet, well, not like what you're used to."

The good news just kept rolling in as Cal brought up something else, "And that's if it was actually sold at a lot in the first place. A lot of the companies around here, rich people or anybody with a fleet of cars, buy directly from KKH, so, even if everybody we talk to cooperates and tells us the truth, which is stretching it, well, we still might not find what we're looking for."

"I don't get this," Jake told his two men. "This morning when I was rolling around in the dirt, your guy, what's his name?"

"Norm," Cal responded.

"Yeah, Norm," Jake went on. "He seemed to think we might have something. Now I don't think I'm that bad at reading people, but I distinctly got the impression that the guy kind of knew what he was doing."

"Well, Deputy," Cal replied, "your people reading skills are right on the money. Norm was a cop here for almost twenty years before he came to work for the CG. He does know his stuff." Before Jake could respond Cal added, "But why he didn't tell you that you were wasting your time is beyond me. He should have known all this right then."

Jake huffed again, "Why is it I get the feeling he did?"

Chapter 11

It felt really strange standing here. It was even stranger how easily they found it. Amy got the address of the warehouse from the report that had been written up by the Germans. They were sticklers for paperwork and protocol. It had barely been twenty minutes after she found out about Danni's shooting when the report about the incident arrived on her computer back at the station. Still, even with that Amy had never expected to find the exact spot where her friend was hit and certainly not as easily as this.

Tony was carefully standing to one side of it as well. Even if neither one of them would say it, both agents acted almost as if it were a desecration to get any closer. They both knew the other was thinking that as well. The only one with a different opinion was Shannon. She would not get any closer to it then Amy's back, which she was practically hiding behind as they all stood there looking down.

It was Tony who said the obvious about the blood-stained cement, "You'd think the rain would have washed some of it away, huh?"

If Tony sounded almost distant it was in stark contrast to Amy's reaction which was pure anger, "You'd think the city would send somebody out here to clean it up. I mean, even some chalk marks or hell, I don't know!" Even a crime scene investigation had a look to it that somehow spelled out officiality. It was not much of a ceremony, but at least it was something. Shouldn't this be important enough for at least that much? To Amy, it just seemed as if her friend had been gutted and then everybody walked away.

Finally, Amy got the shivers and asked Tony yet again, "When's your stupid Aunt supposed to call? I don't want to stand around here any longer than I have too."

"Hey," Tony quipped, "she was nice enough to go digging through all those records for us. That's not to mention what it cost me. I have to go have dinner with them now and do you have idea how bad my Uncle Mac farts?"

Tony walked off in disgust. He temporarily stopped and took a look at the little retaining wall that was closest to the loading docks. He could see how much of the concrete had been chewed and scratched up. It was the telltale sign of bullets slapping soft rock. Tony did not bother to point it out to anyone else. The main reason was because now that he knew how much gun play was involved, he was absolutely astounded that Danni only took two hits and Norm none at all.

Tony's next stop was the loading docks themselves. This place had obviously been empty for a long time, but there were signs of recent activity. He could make out a few footprints and some lines that probably belonged to a load lifter, but the reason he could make them out was due to all the dust that was everywhere else. Then Tony noticed something else and whistled at Amy before telling her, "The door isn't chained. I'm going to have a look around inside."

Amy pointed back to her car and told Shannon, "Go wait for us." For once the kid did not complain. She even looked eager to go sit and wait. It was refreshing, but in Amy's current state of mind, she did not really care for refreshing. She quickly joined Tony, pulled her pistol, switched on her under barrel flashlight, and they both entered the building with weapons at the ready. After a very quick sweep they both lowered their weapons.

Amy grunted in disappointment, "There's nothing here. It's just a great big... empty."

As Tony holstered his weapon back under his jacket, he carefully followed the dust tracks. They led right to an otherwise unremarkable spot where a giant, square impression had been left. The only interesting thing about whatever had been sitting here was that it made more than just an indention in the dust. He squatted down as Amy joined him and then Tony ran his fingers along the floor.

Amy now holstered her weapon and asked, "What is it?"

"Whatever it was," Tony told her, "it was heavy. It actually warped the floor here."

Amy's face became all distorted, "What? Tony, this is a concrete floor. What the hell could warp it?"

Standing back up, Tony wiped the dust from his hands, and told her, "I have

47

no clue, but it didn't just warp it. Hell, it's like it stamped it. The lines are perfectly square, same size as your standard heavy pallet."

All Amy could think to say to that was, "Whatever. It doesn't have a thing to do with why we're here."

"Well, I don't know," Tony replied. "I mean, Danni got shot for a reason. Whatever was in here was worth killing over."

Amy let out a sigh, "For all we know, they got mugged. I'd like to think that if it was something important then Norm would have at least told us that much."

"Oh," Tony raised a brow to that, "is this the same Norman Scoggins that ran off on us and we're now looking for? Tell me, Amy, when's the last time he did that? Hell, normally I can't get the guy off my back and now he's not even taking my calls?"

Both agents reached for their weapons when they heard the telltale signs of stomping feet. Unfortunately, they were almost on Tony and Amy before they even gave away that much. It also turned out that the heavily armed Germans were coming at them from two separate directions. Tony covered the ones coming in by the open loading dock and Amy, standing right beside him, took the ones coming in from the back of the warehouse.

As Tony counted the approaching targets, who also had their weapons raised, he noticed something odd about them. For Wehrmacht they were traveling rather light. Some of them were even armed with pistols instead of assault rifles. Most of them seemed to be missing the body armor that was the usual fair for modern soldiers and a very common sight on the streets around here. Then Tony noticed something even more unusual. Most of these guys appeared to be officers and not enlisted men.

Tony was not really sure what to make of all that, but he was sure he could use it for a little leverage in the here and now. Amy was getting nervous, and despite appearances, so was Tony. Amy could count her side of the equation and knew they were heavily outnumbered and outgunned. Still she asked, "How do we want to play this?"

"Stand your ground," Tony replied with as much force and volume as he could muster. As the Germans stopped in their own L shaped firing line, he hoped at least one of them spoke enough English to understand what he had just told his partner. He repeated it once more just for good measure and then added, "We're not in trouble, yet. Not from these guys anyway."

Then a voice, speaking very good and unaccented English, called out to them from the direction of the loading dock, "Well, if it isn't Agents Tippet and Hiller." Horst came swaggering in following his voice. Unfortunately, he had company with him. He was pushing Shannon along with his riding crop. Tony deflated, lowered his weapon and told Amy, "Ok, now we're in trouble."

Amy lowered her weapon as well. She quickly turned and checked out Shannon. She was relieved to see the teen was not hurt. It did not even appear as if Shannon was scared. If anything, the kid looked pissed as Horst leaned over so he was at eye level with her. He pointed at the agents with his crop and said, "Go join your friends, Miss Reilly." Shannon sneered at him and then walked over to stand next to Tony and Amy. Amy quickly put her arms around the little girl who then complained, "I'm fine already! Will you stop embarrassing me?"

Horst walked out in front of his men and confidently told the two Colonial Agents, "I would say we have something of a standoff, but in order to have that there would have to be two equal sides."

Tony spoke, "So, what are you going to do, Horst? Shoot us? I don't think the Governor would be too happy about that."

"Oh," Horst said lightly, "she might be upset for a couple of days but I'm sure she would live." He kept popping that damn crop in his hand as he paced about. He went on, "Besides, Agent Tippet, why do you think so ill of me? In case you have already forgotten, or perhaps you did not even know, my men are the only reason your friend, Nguyen, is still alive. They were the first on the scene and they were the ones who made sure that she got proper medical attention. For that matter, one of my surgeons was the man who operated on her. I am told she is doing rather well, now."

Amy did not feel hospitable and did not hide that fact when she asked, "What do you want?"

The German shrugged as if what he wanted was nothing at all, "Oh, just some information. I'm sure it will be no bother."

Tony replied to that with, "If we knew anything we wouldn't be here now. Speaking of which, what are you doing here?"

"That is not how this works, Agent Tippet," Horst replied. "I have the advantage, so I get to ask the questions."

Tony laughed at that, "So what are you going to do, Horst? You going to shoot us? You won't get any answers that way. That's what you'd have to do, too, because in case you hadn't noticed" Tony held his pistol up in a non-threatening manner, "I'm still armed and I'm not going to let your guys use their normal methods of interrogation."

The man snorted a quick laugh and replied, "There you go again with the Stalag Seventeen routine. This isn't the twentieth century, Agent Tippet, and if there are any Nazis running around it isn't in the Wehrmacht." Horst stopped pacing. He gave them a sly look and smiled as he pointed to Shannon, "It's more like I was thinking of telling that little girl's mother that you took her to a dangerous crime scene."

Tony's smile evaporated. His weapon hand dropped like a rag doll and he then said, "What do you want to know?"

Horst swaggered over to his quarry. He reached into his jacket for something and Amy flinched. Then he produced what was none other than Shannon's little game. He handed it to the teenager and then he asked Tony, "What is it you plan on doing with Agent Scoggins when you find him?"

Tony blinked, "That's it?"

Horst quickly shot back, "Why would there be anything else?"

The Germans had vanished before they got back to Amy's car which she was happy to see was still in one piece. As Amy slipped in behind the driver's wheel, she did not immediately start the vehicle up. Instead, her head fell back as far as the seat would let it and then with a relieved gasp she said, "Does that guy specialize in scaring the crap out of everybody?"

Tony was not so much worried about that. He was busy thinking. Then he began rambling about the stray facts that were swimming around in his head, "What else is IFOR good at? Amy, did you notice who those guys were?"

She became confused, "Besides being the normal, goose stepping, heavily armed, goon squad that Germans seem to specialize in?"

"That's just it," Tony told her. "That's not who those guys were. That was an intelligence outfit. They got this place under surveillance. I get the feeling they were here doing the same thing we were." Tony then looked into the backseat, "Shannon, when did he take your game console?"

The kid was most definitely still pissed when she answered, "Right after they snatched me out of the car. I dropped it."

Now Amy was less alarmed and more confused, "What's that got to do with anything?"

"Maybe nothing," Tony replied as he reached back and snatched the game away from the teen. Shannon had not bothered with it. The real-life events had completely consumed her and overshadowed the display on her video screen. She still held on to it pretty tight though. Tony only got it out of her hand because she was not expecting him to grab it in the first place. She complained the entire time as he turned it on and then started a new game. Shannon stopped complaining when she realized the sounds coming out of it were not the usual music that she was so accustomed to.

After they finished listening, Tony stated the obvious, "Horst wasn't trying to get information from us. He was trying to tell us something."

"I don't get it," Amy replied. "Why give us this? Why point guns at us and give us this? What does he care?"

Tony snickered and replied, "Cause he's looking for the same thing as the rest of us, only he can't do it without raising the alarm."

Now Amy was becoming very nervous, "We need to go back to the station and tell Cal or the new guy, somebody!"

"No," Tony replied. "I think I know why Norm is ducking us now. If I'm right, and well if he's right, then we can't tell anybody." Before Amy could protest Tony put up his hands and said, "At least not yet. Think about it, Amy. All this starts happening right when the new guy gets here. What's that all about?"

Amy slid down her seat and it was appropriate because she had quite the sinking feeling. Tony only added to her paranoia, "We don't know a thing about this Barton guy. For all we know, he's just an American spook that they sent here to spy on us."

"Barbara said," Amy replied in a very pale voice that matched her current complexion, "the guy used to be a green beret."

"And he didn't show up at Riggins this morning," Tony followed. "And where does he say he was? Over at the consulate, right? How do we know that, or for that matter, is it such a good thing that he was eating breakfast with Whitman?"

"Good point," Amy so wished Tony was not making sense.

Shannon, on the other hand, was alive and excited, "So, where do we go next?"

Tony grumbled at that, "You're going to stay with my aunt till we get this sorted out."

"Like hell I will," the fourteen-year-old replied.

That promptly snapped Amy back to reality, "Watch your mouth. What if your mother heard that?"

"Mom's not here." Shannon went on by saying, "And if you drop me off somewhere, I'm going to tell everybody everything that just happened."

Tony snapped at the kid, "This isn't a game, Shannon."

"Look Tony," Shannon bit back with no less resolve. "I'm sick of this innocent little kid crap. I don't know if you guys have noticed, but the whole Arch is dangerous. Look, Danni was my friend, too. I want to plug the sorry bastards just as much as you do."

Amy was cross-eyed, "Shannon, it was a mistake bringing you here in the first place. I'm not going to…"

Shannon cut her off with, "I'll tell mom what you and surfer boy have been doing out on the beach every night."

Amy started the car, "So where to next?"

Chapter 12

Jake almost wanted to moan when he looked across what passed for a major highway. Garcia had driven him here because Jake still had no idea where anything was. He had not even spent five hours on this rock yet and the disasters seemed to be piling up faster than the hours. The only good news here was that at least everything was convenient. Jake pointed it out to his driver, "That's the place that went up in smoke this morning?"

Garcia put the car in park and then looked at what the new boss was talking about, "What? You mean Foo King? Yeah, that's it all right." Then Garcia pointed to the little strip mall they were at, "The dry cleaners are right there."

"If I had known this place was here this morning," Jake replied, "I could have saved myself the trouble." That seemed to be the biggest problem he had right now too. Jake had no idea where anything was or how anything worked in these parts. He was completely dependent on other people for even the most basic of services. and to an old Special Forces guy, that just smelled plain wrong. That went doubly so when he was sure someone else was using it against him.

What choice did Jake have? This little trip was a prime example of that. Jake had worn his best suit when he came down from the starship. He had figured the day would start out with meeting all the high officials, and never once did he dream, he would be playing in the sand box. Jake still had a few more officials to go too. The most important of which was meeting the Governor for dinner this evening. He could not do that in the blue pilots' jumpsuit he was currently wearing.

Jake had borrowed it from the station, and not because his suit was the only thing he had to wear, but right now Jake wanted something a little more official looking than jeans. The jumpsuit not only fit, but had a badge stenciled on it. That would have to do until he got a real badge, a newly minted phone with his identification cards and all the other little things that went with being duly checked in. That could not happen until after he met with the Governor, unfortunately. That was why he was now at the dry cleaners.

When Jake came back out and got back in the car, he told Garcia, "Drive me over there."

Garcia was busy with his phone, "Hey, I just got an update text from Kaiser."

It took a second for Jake to realize what the guy was talking about, "Oh, the hospital. How's she doing?"

Garcia sounded relieved, "She's awake."

"Not bad for a few hours," Jake mumbled and then pointed once again to the diner, "Now, let's go back over to the crime scene." He also now had one other place he wanted to go, and he still had very limited time to do it all in. Garcia promptly did as instructed, and after a few almost near mishaps with other traffic, did finally manage to get them back to the diner. Jake was a little surprised to see the place was open for business again. He was equally surprised to see that cars were already parking over the burn marks from this morning's fiasco.

Leaving Garcia in the car, Jake found the guy with all the supplies right back at his window as if nothing had ever happened. When Jake said as much to the guy, whose name he thought was Mel, the guy took offense, "Look pal, a good friend of mine got killed this morning. Her name was Grace and she left behind two orphaned kids. So, no, my morning is not going along with business as usual." Mel also added from behind his window, "In fact, I knew things were pretty screwed up when Gracie first came and pointed that truck out to me."

That took Jake by surprise, "She waited on it? Did she say anything?"

"Stuff that was none of her business," Mel replied. "I tried to steer her away from it. That guy was trouble, although I got to admit, I didn't expect the kind we got."

Jake's brows narrowed, "You knew the guy?"

"Knew of him. Hell, everybody in the Arch does," Mel replied. He also added, "And it couldn't have happened to a nicer guy."

"Um," Jake thought about it for a minute and did have a question that he stumbled to get out, "you're going to have to forgive me but…"

"You're new here," Mel finished the sentence. "You stick out like a sour

54

thumb, buddy."

"Don't you mean sore?"

"Not in my line of work," Mel replied. He then went on, "The guy's name is Roy. It's Roy Kingsley. That mean anything to you?"

"Not particularly," Jake replied, "no." That was not entirely true but close enough. It was certainly more than Mel needed to know. "Is he important?"

That caught a condescending laugh from the cook who then said, "Of the Texian Legion Kingsleys. I'm sure you heard of them all the way back to Earth."

The one question that Jake did ask this time had nothing to do with anything about the case, "How did you know I was from Earth?"

"The accent," Mel replied. "I heard a lot of it in the military. Speaking of which, like I was telling that buddy of yours, I seen me one or two explosions back during the war. That one wasn't like none I ever seen short of a nuke. Only not quite as big. You know what I mean?"

Jake nodded to the man as he walked off and said, "More than you realize." When he got back to the car, Jake noticed that Garcia was still busy with his phone, so, Jake asked him, "Hear anything else?"

"Just letting everybody know," Garcia replied. For a moment, Jake wondered if he should stop the guy. Then Jake decided against it. The girl was their friend after all. They deserved to know and anything else was of secondary importance. Garcia finished quickly enough anyway. He probably already had blabbed it to half the island by now. When Garcia was done, he did ask, "Did you find out anything else?"

Jake repeated the question he had been asked, "Does the name Roy Kingsley mean anything to you?"

Garcia coughed and then said, "He was behind this?"

"Sort of," Jake replied, "but it was more like right in the middle. He was the guy in the truck."

Garcia coughed again and then said, "Roy was the schmuck who got vaporized? I don't know if we need to arrest who did it or pin a medal on the guy."

That answered Jake's next question of, "Who would want to kill the man?" Judging by what Garcia had just said the answer was, everybody. Instead of asking the question, Jake just watched as the agent pulled his phone back out and readied up his thumbs to type. Jake snatched the phone away from him. "Till we close this case you keep your mouth shut, and your fingers too for that matter."

Garcia was not sure exactly how to take that. He just stared at Jake until the man told him, "Drive!"

In a meek voice Garcia replied, "Can I have my phone back?" There was no answer all the way to the hospital. There wasn't much of any talking at all for that matter. The next thing that was said as they rode the elevator up to the Intensive Care Unit was Garcia pointing out, "They're not going to let us see her."

"Are we not cops?" Jake thought about it and corrected himself, "Ok, I'm not officially a cop yet, but are you not a cop?"

Garcia was confused, "What difference does that make? No disrespect, um, deputy, it's just that the CG doesn't carry a whole lot of weight around here. You ask anybody with the city, or hell even the Wehrmacht, and the answer is going to be…"

The doors opened and Jake cut in with, "Get out."

"Something like that," Garcia replied.

When they reached the doors to the ICU, they found themselves with the exact trouble that Garcia had expected. The woman at the outside counter would not buzz them in. She was a cranky woman and kept saying, "We cannot let our patients be disturbed. They're in there for a reason."

"Look, lady," Jake told her. "I'm a Deputy US Marshall and this here is an Agent of your own Government. We are conducting an official investigation here."

The woman was unimpressed. She looked to Garcia as she pointed at Jake, "Alvarez, who is this butt munch?"

Garcia felt like, and was in reality, kind of on the spot, "He's who he says he is, Kitty. He's a Deputy US Marshall. He's also kind of our new boss."

Kitty acted impressed as she looked back to Jake, but she also made it apparent that her admiring glare was all sarcasm, "Oh, one of those treaty people from Earth come here to save all us poor little colonists from ourselves." Then her glare turned downright hostile, "Kind of like the cock sucker they sent here to run this place."

Jake just nodded, "Yeah, that would be me. Now while you're feeling all self-righteous, Kitty," and Jake made the name sound as sarcastic as he could. Then he got downright hostile, "I got a kid sitting in there with a few extra holes in her body and I'm kind of interested in finding the real cock suckers who did it to her. So why don't you get off your fat, lazy ass and push the damn button so we can go find out if she remembers what they look like."

The woman was red-faced, livid, and had yet to unlock her eyes with those of Jake. She did, however, reach over and hit the button. As the two men walked off, Kitty left one parting thought, "Good luck, Alvarez. You're going to need it."

When the ICU doors closed behind them, Garcia suddenly exploded, "Holy shit! I never seen anybody talk to her like that." As an afterthought he added, "And live."

"It's a front, kid," Jake told him as he looked around in the many little cubicles for patients. "She's just another bureaucrat who's too lazy to push a button and then fill out the forms that come with it." He finally had to ask a nurse who fortunately proved to be more helpful than Kitty. The guy led them right to Danni's little space.

Danni was not only awake but she instantly recognized Garcia and smiled. He slid into a chair next to her bed and took the girl's hand. Jake just stood back and watched as they exchanged the kind of comments you normally expected in such situations. That included the nurse warning Garcia about all the needles that were currently sticking in Danni's hand.

Jake took that as his cue, "Agent Nguyen, if you're finished giving Agent Alvarez a hard-on, I'd like to chat with you for a moment."

For some reason Danni did not look confused at all. She simply directed her attention at the man, and with a weak sounding voice she stated, "Pretty good accent for a German."

Garcia corrected her, "He's our new boss."

Jake cut her off at the pass. He knew how pain meds could be, and better than most, "Yeah, I'm the cock sucker."

That sent the girl into a giggling fit that ended in some rather harsh sounding coughs. When she could speak again, she said, "He reads minds, too."

Jake just kept it simple, "What happened, Agent? How did you get shot?"

Danni fell asleep a couple of times as she tried to get things straight. Finally, it was the nurse that put an end to it. Jake let the guy because it was quite clear the man was only doing it for reasons involving Danni's health. Jake nodded for Garcia, who smiled at Danni one last time, and they both left the ICU. When they were out the door Garcia just shrugged, "Hate to tell you I told you so, man. Nothing she said helped one little bit."

"Yeah, it did," Jake told him. Then he looked to his man and said, "Who is this Sally Henchersfield?"

Chapter 13

"Are you sure this," Amy had to think about it again, "Sally..."

Shannon finished the name in a glib tone, "Henchersfield." Then Shannon stuck her phone over the seat so that Amy could get a firsthand look at its screen, "This is where the phone book says she lives." When Amy still looked unconvinced the teen got the idea that it was not because of the address. Shannon repeated her earlier argument, "You heard my game. If Danni said she met with this girl last night, then it's obvious she had something to do with it."

Amy also knew that in the recording, probably made by a German observation post over by the warehouse, Danni had also mentioned that they met with some guy. None of it made any sense, and so Amy was still not convinced that they were doing anything more than wasting their time.

Tony had not let his eyes drift off the house since they pulled up in front of it and parked. It was not exactly a mansion, but it probably cost more than any three homes that Tony had ever lived in, combined. Amy did not say as much, but then again, did she really have too? What she did ask was the question that was primarily on Tony's mind, "You said she was in Danni's class? That would make her what?"

"I don't know," Tony shrugged. "What, twenty-three, twenty-four maybe?"

All Amy could say to that was, "What does she do for a living?"

Shannon was more than a little excited, "I know! Maybe she's like a high-end prostitute!"

Both adults looked back at the kid and then Amy said, "Who keeps filling your mind with all this smut?"

Shannon shrugged it off, "I don't know. I mean, did you see what Danni was wearing when she left the station last night? It was almost less than what you two had…"

"That's enough," Tony said putting up his hand. He was particularly miffed because they had a serious problem that the nice amenities of the house had almost caused him to overlook. He pointed to the front door, "I'd call that a problem."

Amy sighed, "It's busted in. Oh, this day is turning out to be just peachy."

Shannon became confused, "What's peachy?"

Tony ignored the kid, "With a house like this, it's a sure-fired bet there's an alarm system."

"Which means," Amy added, "it just happened." She looked to the teenager. "I mean it this time. Stay in the car."

Amy did not wait to draw her weapon this time. It was out before she even got her feet planted firmly on the ground. Tony was obviously quicker. He was already running for the back of the house before Amy could even reach the front yard, let alone cross it. Since there was a brick staircase almost as tall as she was, Amy had a little trouble getting to the door. She did not like going straight at it so that left her stomping through some bushes and then climbing up the railing before she could make it inside. By the time she entered, what proved to be a living room, she heard some muffled cries coming from further in the house.

Amy called out, "Miss Hen.. Hen… Sally?"

It was Tony that replied, "You're clear. Get back here."

Amy felt a little relieved when she entered the dining room/ kitchen area. Tony was standing there, and he looked relaxed enough, so Amy lowered her weapon but did not put it away. Then she looked at the source of the noise she heard. It was definitely not Sally unless the woman had somehow turned into a man. The guy was no less in dire need as someone had handcuffed him to a banister rail and then taped his eyes and mouth shut.

Amy kind of shrugged, "Boyfriend maybe?"

"I don't think so," Tony replied. He then nodded towards the back door, "Looks the same back there as it did up front. They came in from two directions from the looks of it, and maybe even three. I think there's a window out upstairs."

Amy reached over and ripped the tape off the guys eyes. He looked at her with panic, but when he looked at Tony, there was something else there. Amy could have sworn it was recognition, maybe? No matter what their bound and helpless guy thought of him, it was clear that Tony did indeed recognize the guy. Tony said as much as Amy tore the tape off the guy's mouth, "Well, if it isn't Fast Finger Freddy."

At first the guy was about to say something less than cordial, but then he stopped and looked at Amy in shock, "That hurt!" Finally, he turned his attention on Tony, "And you know I hate that fucking name, Tony! My name is Frank! NOT FRED!"

Amy shrugged so Tony explained, "He's my second cousin." Then he turned his attention back to the guy, "So, you got caught good this time, Freddy? I told you, getting nicked by the city was the least of your problems."

"I did not get nicked, you sanctimonious moron," Frank replied. "I'm the victim here! I was just minding my own business…"

Amy added, "In somebody else's living room."

Frank rattled on as if she had never said a word, "When out of nowhere, some crazy paramedic comes out of the shadows like he's Spiderman..."

Tony winced, "Shadows? It's the middle of the day, Freddy."

Amy added, "In somebody else's living room in the middle of the day."

Tony calmly asked, "How long you been here, Freddy?"

"FRANK," he protested, "and I don't know. I mean, it was early this morning before the sun came up. That's all I know. Now are you two going to let me go so I can go piss or do I have to do it my pants."

Tony and Amy both looked at his zipper and noted the stain. Tony was the one who said it, "Kind of looks like you emptied your bladder already. Was that when the ambulance driver got you or after?"

"After!" Frank went on with, "Bozo! And I didn't say he was an ambulance driver. I said paramedic, ok?"

Amy crossed her arms, "And you knew this how?"

"He had on scrubs," Gary replied. "You know the kind they wear in that old doctor's show, um, what was it called?"

Tony answered, "Scrubs."

"Yeah, that's the one," Frank replied.

Amy then asked, "And did you happen to see this guy's face?"

"I told you it was dark," Frank told her. Then he remembered, "Well, he was a black guy. I remember that much."

Amy continued, "So, then he just busted in the door and drug you in here and handcuffed you to this rail?"

"No," Frank sneered. "That would be stupid. The door was already busted in when I first.. I mean, when I was walking by."

Tony nodded and Amy followed him back out to the front yard and far

61

enough away that they could no longer hear Frank screaming. Standing on the walkway, Tony told her, "Well, I believe part of his story." When he got a strange look from Amy he pointed out, "Well, he didn't break in both doors and everything is still in the house."

Amy sighed and she could also read between the lines, "You think Norm did it?"

"I think whoever broke in those doors had come and gone before Norm even got here," Tony told her with a hint of frustration. He then added with a nod to the house, "And why would Norm bust in both doors? Whoever went in that place knew what they were doing and had more than a few people."

"Yeah, but," Amy was confused, "why would the Germans do it? I mean, Horst all but led us here."

"If it was even him in the first place," Tony added. He did have to admit that, "Well, we know Horst knew about this girl and he'd have less trouble tracking her down than we would."

Now Amy was suddenly not so worried about tracking down Sally Whatshername. She looked in the car and it was empty, "Where's Shannon?"

It was Shannon who answered as she came walking out of the house, "And you guys call yourselves cops." The kid rolled her eyes, "You were so busy with Lame Ass Side Show in there you missed the real attraction."

Suddenly Tony became very concerned until Shannon pulled her hands out from behind her back. She handed Amy the first object which was a framed picture. Amy wanted to be shocked but could not make herself be. She showed the photo to Tony who recognized two of the three girls in the picture. Danni was obvious and the other girl with the brown hair was none other than Natasha Ivanov. Tony pointed at the picture with the triumph that came with being right, "I told you she had a flat chest!"

Amy groaned and said, "The point is, that's the woman that came to the hospital a little while ago. That's Tasha Kingsley!"

Shannon smirked and raised her nose in condescension, "And I'm guessing the blond is Sally."

Amy still kept on frowning, "Fat lot of good it does us. We still don't know where Norm is and we can add this Sally chick to the list of missing persons."

Why was Tony smiling? He held up the object that Shannon had handed him. It was a white name plate with 'SALLY' written on it. There was smaller writing beneath it. Tony saved Amy the trouble of reading it, "Doctor Cashton's office. Sally is the receptionist."

Amy's mind was obviously not on her work. She was quite ticked when she blurted out, "A fucking secretary can afford a place like this!"

Shannon snickered, "Told you she was a call girl."

Tony was smug, "You don't get it, do you?" He held up the photo again and pointed to just beneath Natasha's neckline. Amy couldn't help but get the feeling that Tony was trying to rub her boobs, but then she forgot all about that when he said, "He's a plastic surgeon."

Chapter 14

The rain had stopped so it was an opportune time to open up the doors in the study and have some tea on the back patio. That was what Mrs. Kingsley thought at any rate. She never bothered to ask her husband what his opinion was. It did not matter. Hyrum found himself sitting at the table with her anyway. He did what he always had to in such situations. He sat beside her and patiently waited for the servants while he smiled at his wife. He was even smiling when she pointed across the back lawn and asked him, "Is that the new gardener, dear?"

At first, Hyrum had no idea what she was talking about, but then his eyes caught sight of the man in the blue jean jacket and sloppy shirt. The guy was just casually strolling across the lawn like he belonged here, even if Hyrum knew better. What was even more important was that Hyrum's security man, Baxter, saw the guy too. His hand slipped into his jacket, but Hyrum gave the man a nervous shake of the head and the bodyguard eased off. Hyrum subtly checked to make sure that his wife had not seen Baxter overreact. Fortunately, she seemed none the wiser.

Norm stopped just shy of the table and was all smiles, "Been a long time, Hyrum."

No matter how civil Hyrum could act, he could not bring himself to smile at this man. He did give yet another nod to Baxter just to make sure the guy knew to back off. Security types were never known for thinking beyond the moment.

Myra Kingsley became excited, "Oh, you know Hyrum?" She graciously looked to her husband, "Why, you didn't tell us we were having guests? It's such an opportune time."

"Why, so it is," Hyrum Kingsley almost had to bite his tongue when he said that. He invited Norman to sit down, "Next time you must call."

"Yeah," Norman replied, "I know what a busy schedule you have." Norman shot a glance at Baxter who was behind Mrs. Kingsley and hence showed no effort to display civility. Norm went on, "But I always somehow manage to drop by when I get the chance."

Hyrum's eyes narrowed, "And here I was thinking you were stuck up on the north shore. Bad weather today, Norm. You might have a little difficulty getting back."

Myra was even more excited, "Oh, do you work with Hyrum? He never talks about his work and I find it just so delightful to hear stories."

Norm chuckled and told the man's wife, "We travel in the same circles, Mrs. Kingsley. Oh, I'd say me and your husband go way back." Then he looked right at Hyrum and said, "And as for getting back, let's just say we all get rained on. That storm I got caught up in is just as liable to come your way."

Hyrum chuckled and replied, "A smart man has got sense enough to come in out of the rain."

"My last house had some leaks," Norm shot back.

Mrs. Kingsley told him, "Oh, we know a very good contractor."

Norm nodded to the woman who seemed to be very good at remaining gracious. Norm could never figure out how she managed it so well after being married to this asshole for so long. He told the lady, "It's funny you should mention that, Mrs. Kingsley. It's that very thing that's brought me by here today. I am told that Hyrum knows people that can get all kinds of things fixed."

Hyrum was not as giddy as his wife when he said, "So, are you trying to tell me that your house sprung a leak?"

"Actually," Norm replied, "I think it's one of those properties that we have a mutual interest in." Norm managed another polite chuckle as his eyes wandered back up to the security guard. The guy had reached inside his coat, and for a moment, Norm was really concerned that the guy might just draw. It was only a servant walking by that seemed to stop him.

The strange thing was that, after a moment, Norm was not so sure that the servant was the reason for Baxter's hesitation. It was almost as if it was the phone that Hyrum got. After a moment of listening to the call, Hyrum got right up and said, "I have to take this call." The bodyguard wanted to follow, but Hyrum made it very clear, "You keep the lady company, Mr. Baxter." Of course, Norman heard it as, "Watch that son of a bitch and kill him if he moves." There was little doubt that was what the old man meant. The bodyguard was not happy, but he obeyed, and Norm made sure he never let his sight off the man.

Mrs. Kingsley seemed oblivious to all of it. She was sitting at a very bad angle if one wanted to see what was going on around them. It made Norm wonder if that was how she handled her entire life. Unlike her husband, the lady seemed genuine. "You know I must apologize. When I first saw you, I thought you were the new gardener. We've had such a terrible time with my roses that I just had to hire on a new man. In my defense, he was supposed to be here today."

Norm had seen a pattern now. This Baxter guy wanted to be in two places at once and he was having a hard time making up his mind which one it should be. He got very nervous when Hyrum walked back into his study. Baxter kept looking back, even stepping closer to the open door, while trying to keep as much of his attention focused on Norm as he could. Norm decided to divide the guy's attention even more.

"You know Mrs. Kingsley," he told her. "My father had quite a green thumb. He taught me all kinds of things about flower beds. You know we have such poor soil around here and the really important thing is making sure you have the right mulch in the ground."

"Oh," she was excited, "I do wish you would take a look at mine."

That got Baxter's undivided attention, "Mrs. Kingsley, maybe we should wait until your husband gets back before…"

She was already on her feet when she paid her first attention to the bodyguard, "Oh poo, Hyrum's in there hours sometimes." She looked to Norm, "I would be more than honored if you would look at my roses." As they walked off towards the garden, and the back wall that Norm had crawled over to get in here, Norm made sure he put his hand behind his back and extended a proper middle finger for Baxter. Now that the guy was torn between two impossible tasks, he did what most guys like him always do in such circumstances, nothing at all.

When Hyrum finally did get back, he was furious, "Where is my wife?!"

"Um, Sir," Baxter stumbled over his words, "she insisted!"

"Those damn roses," Hyrum knew exactly what this was all about. He looked back towards the garden and a few minutes later his wife came out, alone. She waved at him, was happy with a smile on her face, and was getting down on her knees to play in the mud. Now that he knew she was safe, Hyrum growled at his security man, "Find out how that son of a bitch got in here."

"Um," Baxter pulled at his collar and asked, "don't you want us to go after him?"

"He's halfway to downtown by now," Hyrum replied in a biting tone. After a moment he noticed that Baxter was still standing there. Hyrum barked this time, "Well, go do what you're told, boy!"

When the guard was gone, Hyrum pulled his phone back out of his pocket. As he watched his wife play in the garden, he hit a speed dial number and then told the person that answered, "Where the hell is my son?"

Hyrum was not sure which was worse, the constant and never-ending flow of gracious optimism from his wife or the never-ending sobs from the girl on the phone. She was so bad she started coughing before she answered him, "I don't know. I was on the phone with him this morning and we were cut off. He never called me back."

With no ceremony, not even so much as a goodbye, Hyrum disconnected and then tried calling Roy Kingsley one more time. All he got was the same recording that he did the first time around. The feminine sounding electronic voice told him that the party could not be reached. This time Hyrum hung up with a curse on his lips.

It was not unheard of for Roy to miss an appointment. It was certainly not unlike him to ignore his phone. Roy was even prone to fits of not calling his old man for days at a time. What was disturbing was that Roy was doing it now. Hyrum had to think long and hard before he finally figured out what to do. It was not what he wanted to do, but as of right now, he saw where there was little choice.

This time when a voice sounded on the other end of the phone, Hyrum Kingsley was hard and authoritative when he said, "I want to speak to Chief Summers, please, and don't pawn me off on one of his flunkies. This is Hyrum Kingsley calling."

Chapter 15

Garcia came walking up the driveway with two sacks in his hands. He held one up for Calvin who took a quick sniff of the air around the bag and then gestured to have it taken away, preferably by a hazmat team. Garcia laughed, "Come on, bro, you don't know good eating when you see it."

"Seeing isn't the problem," Cal then took a step away from his fellow agent and waved for him to leave.

Garcia ignored him and then motioned to the Deputy Marshall who was busy with some box on the side of the house, "What is he doing?"

"I have no clue," Cal told him.

Jake, on the other hand, answered the question by pointing out he was capable, "You know, I am standing in earshot."

Cal just shrugged, "You looked busy."

Jake dropped the metal cover back over the box and walked back to his men. He began sniffing and then mumbled, "Must be another one of those armored things." After that he picked up the volume as he began wiping the dust off his hands, "You guys set a new record for primitive on this rock. I don't think I've ever seen a security system like that one outside of a museum."

As Jake walked around to the front of the house with his guys in tow, he decided to give up on explaining the finer points of home security systems. It was pretty clear that the one he had just finished inspecting could have been disarmed by anyone with a minimal level of training. He walked past the busted front door and stopped in a position where he could see most of the lower floor.

Then Jake gave his synopsis, "This place has been like grand central station today."

Garcia laughed and then nodded to the broken front door. He sarcastically commented, "Don't know what would give you that idea."

Jake was not amused, "Those doors, the front and the back, were taken off by steel battering rams." When Jake just got a couple of shrugs he pointed out, "Well if you're going to come in that way there really isn't much point in disabling the security system. Everybody in the whole neighborhood is going to hear you coming. You don't need an alarm to wake everybody up. Besides that, anybody that does that doesn't care if everybody knows they're here and who does that?"

"Cops," Garcia replied.

Cal corrected him, "I was thinking more like the Wehrmacht."

"Exactly," Jake said as he pointed to Cal. Then he pointed up, "And whoever came in upstairs was a whole different crew. They're the ones who cut the security alarm off. Since the door breech didn't set off any alarm that means the upstairs guys were here first."

Garcia finally set down his takeout food and then he commented, "This Sally chick is a popular girl."

"Oh, it gets even better than that," Jake replied. He pointed to a banister rail between the kitchen and dining room, "Somebody was handcuffed to that pole. From the looks of the scrapes it was probably all morning. I'm guessing he came in after the Germans and that means we got two other sets of visitors."

Cal assumed a thoughtful pose before stating, "I'm not following."

Jake just shrugged, "Somebody had to cuff him to the pole and he obviously couldn't get loose. He was blindfolded and gagged, too."

Garcia was becoming skeptical, "Now, how can you know that?" After the look he got back from Jake, the agent back-pedaled a little by adding, "Sir."

Jake just shook his head and then pointed to the floor, "Cause the duct tape is sitting right over there, genius."

Now Cal was getting it, "Which means somebody else had to come in and cut him loose." Cal sighed and then went on, "This leaves us with one tiny little problem, deputy. The only home wreckers we've been able to identify so far, are the ones we can't do anything about. You hit the nail on the head when you figured that Horst and his boys don't care if anyone knew they were here. They don't care because there isn't anything we can do about it."

"Unfortunately, Agent Brandt," Jake replied, "our German buddies may be the least of our problems right now." Both men waited for Jake to continue so he just said it, "Whoever came in upstairs knew more about what they were doing than the Wehrmacht goon squad." It still did not seem to penetrate so Jake spelled it out, "Your typical infantry grunt is a bulldozer. He goes right at the target with all the power he's got. It's as messy as that front door. A special ops unit is another matter."

Cal felt a shiver run up his spine, "So, what you're trying to tell me is that whoever came here first was…"

"Special Forces," Jake replied.

Garcia's mouth dropped open and then he said, "We got a new player in town." Then he got angry because there was nothing else he could do. Then he went into denial and said, "That doesn't make any sense. What did you say this girl was, Cal? A fucking receptionist? What would some roger ramjet green berets want to go jacking up a glorified secretary for?"

Jake took another look around the home. There were some pretty nice things in here and that was not even counting the house itself. That sent him back upstairs to the bedroom where he began browsing around the room. Jake noticed that only Cal followed him this time. When Jake found some pictures on a shelf, he handed one of them to Cal and said, "Well, there's the connection we already knew about."

It was a picture of five girls at some bar. One of them was most obviously Danni. Cal put it back on the shelf and just silently watched the new boss. The man

69

was just staring silently at yet another picture. Just before Cal was going to ask him, he volunteered the information and tossed the other picture over, "I think that answers the question of how she paid for this place."

This picture only had two people in it, if you did not count the guy in the giant chipmunk suit. It was a young blond-headed girl and some middle-aged guy. Cal recognized where the picture was taken. It was at a resort about three islands over. Cal laughed when he thought of it. When he got a look from Jake he said, "Oh, it's nothing. I just always told my wife I was going to take her to this place one day."

Jake raised a brow, "I thought you lived in the barracks?"

"I do," Cal replied as he put the picture back up. "Divorced." Then he volunteered, "Probably because I never actually got around to taking her there."

Now Jake had his thinking face back on, "What do you want to bet the guy in that picture is her boss. Didn't you say she worked for some doctor?"

"Yeah," Cal nodded. "One of the top plastic surgeons on the island, too." That struck a note with Jake, but Cal was not sure why, "I've never heard anything about Cashton being dirty. What are you thinking?"

Jake just shrugged, "I don't know. We don't have a lot here to go on. It's just that this doctor guy has enough money to have a wife and a girlfriend, at least I'm assuming he's married. I know that Nguyen kept saying, back in the hospital, that Sally called her, but it didn't sound like Sally was the one who wanted to do the talking."

Now Cal was a bit befuddled, "To Cashton?"

Again, Jake just shrugged, "Maybe he got in some trouble. His girlfriend knows a cop and so he gets this Sally to hook them up."

Cal just shook his head, "And this brings down the green berets and the SS goon squad? I don't know, deputy. That sounds pretty ridiculous."

"The problem here is," Jake told him, "we don't know everything, so sure it's going to look ridiculous. Look at it from the point of view of what we do know. Somebody shot Nguyen and it's looking more and more like it was because she stumbled into something. Whatever that something is has caught the attention of the Germans, and I can assure you, guys like Horst don't get theirs hands dirty unless they're getting some serious goodies out of it."

"So, it's big," Cal added. He just shrugged, "So what? That doesn't help us very much."

"Yeah, it does," Jake replied. "For one thing it narrows down our list of suspects. The only people who are playing in this ball court are pros and there aren't that many of them around. We also know," he pointed to the broken window, "that they all want this Sally pretty bad. That gives us an advantage because they don't know where she is either."

"Now, wait a minute," Cal came back with. "How do you know she isn't already fish food? You're the one saying we're dealing with some kind of military black ops unit. How good is a secretary going to do against that?" As an afterthought he added, "And Horst, too, while we're at it."

"Not much of one, but," Jake replied, "you see this nice expensive house this girl's got. I guess she must have an expensive car to go with it. What kind was it?"

"How should I know?" Cal thought about it and with some agitation he said in an almost accusing tone, "Wait a minute. The driveway is empty. How would you even kn…" Suddenly it hit Cal and he saw Jake's face light up when it did. Cal let out a short laugh and said, "She wasn't home."

Jake nodded in appreciation and then said, "And the logical place to check next is her job."

Cal bowed in an appreciative way and gestured to the stairs, "After you, sir."

When they reached the front door, they found Garcia standing in the splinters of wood that used to be the front door and looking out. He pointed to the curb and asked Jake, "Friends of yours?"

Jake let a silent but audible, "Oh, crap." Then he walked on out to meet Gary Moss who was standing with two other black suited men with sunglasses. Moss took his shades off when Jake stopped in front of him. In an easy and friendly kind of way, Moss commented, "Well, you've had a busy first day, Major."

Jake got right to it, "Is there a point to this little visit, Moss? Did Whitman forget to have me sign some papers or something?"

"Actually, Jake," Moss replied, "I'm here to keep you out of trouble. It seems we might have a little scandal brewing and Consul Whitman has ordered me to come and save your ass. It just wouldn't look good for the United States if our newest treaty guy winds up in hot water when he hasn't even presented his credentials yet."

Jake sized up the right-hand and left-hand man. Then he asked the simple question, "And if I say no?"

"You won't, Jake," Moss replied. "I think you're going to want to see what I have to show you."

Chapter 16

Amy sat on the hood of her car and watched Shannon with an eagle eye. The girl seemed to resent it even if she would occasionally smile and wave back from the line she was standing in on the inside of the Foo King Junior restaurant. It was incredibly slow going in there, but right now Amy did not care. She looked over to Tony who was standing by a nearby light pole in the diner's parking lot. He too had his phone to his ear, and from the looks of it his aunt had him on hold.

Meanwhile Amy was also stuck listening to elevator music until a woman's voice came on the other line and said, "This is Eleanor, may I help you?"

Amy put on her best drawl as she replied, "Howdy, ma'am. I'm Mrs. Kingsley's personal assistant and I just so need to talk with Miss Sally, really I do."

"I'm sorry but she's not in today," the woman on the line replied. Then she went on with, "Did you say you're Myra Kingsley's assistant?"

"Oh, good gracious, no," Amy told the woman. "I'm Miss Tasha's assistant."

There was a short pause and Amy got the feeling that the woman did not believe her. This Eleanor sounded extremely skeptical, but when she came back on, she did seem, at least a little, more relaxed, "That might explain why I've never talked with you before."

"Well, I am kind of new," Amy replied and then winced when she realized that even she did not believe her own accent.

"So, am I to understand," Eleanor asked, "that Mrs. Kingsley, Tasha that is, wants to see Dr. Cashton now, too? She will need an initial consultation, you do understand that, right?"

Amy was a bit confused by that, but she went on, "Is there any way we can get Miss Tasha in there today? You do understand that she has quite the schedule."

"I'm afraid that's impossible," Eleanor explained. "He's booked up for the next two months solid."

"Well, now," Amy came back with, "you know Mrs. Kingsley can make it well worth the doctor's time, if you know what I mean. She's good like that and all."

There was yet another pause and then Eleanor finally said, "We might be able to get her in after hours in a few days. I'm afraid I couldn't schedule anything sooner. The doctor is out of town right now."

"I will be so sure to discuss this with Mrs. Kingsley," then Amy added just before hanging up, "Y'all be good, ya here?" She took a deep breath and then spit as if the accent were a bad taste in her mouth. She also found that Tony had finished his conversation and slipped up on her. She saw the strange, almost stoic, look that he was giving her, "What?"

Tony tried to imitate her, "Y'all be good, ya here?"

"Shut up," Amy said with a swat to his arm. Then she asked, "Did your aunt find anything out?"

"Well, I can guess why Horst was so interested in the building now," Tony told her. "Like a lot of those warehouses over there, it's owned by a company with an e-mail address and not much more."

Amy nodded, "So it's Texas Mob."

"Probably," Tony replied. "It's starting to look more and more like Danni and Norm walked into a drug shipment in progress. Only…"

Amy shrugged, "Only what?"

"What kind of drugs leave dents in concrete floors?"

It was a perfectly legitimate question and one that Amy had to admit she had no answer for. She also saw it as somewhat irrelevant now. Her own lead was looking more and more like a dead end and that meant they had no place left to go. She told Tony what she had found out and that left him thinking hard.

Then Tony said, "You mean Natasha wasn't a patient of his?"

"Didn't sound like it," Amy replied. Then she snapped, "And don't you say you wonder who did her tits or I'm going to really slap you this time."

Tony did not even act as if he noticed Amy's rebuke. He then stated rhetorically, "And Cashton isn't there either. Don't you find that a little coincidental? I'm willing to bet that he was the guy Danni met with last night."

Amy rolled her eyes, "No shit, Sherlock. It still doesn't leave us any place left to go with this. I say we call Cal and tell him what we've found."

"Not till we've found Norm," Tony was still convinced he had to keep this compartmentalized. If they told one person at the station, then everybody was likely to find out and that meant the new guy too. "We do have one place left to go. We need a look at Cashton's records."

Amy's face distorted, "Why?"

"Cause I'm starting to think we're looking for the wrong person," Tony told her. "Sally just knew Danni and that she was a cop. Don't you get it, Amy? She hooked-up Cashton. He's the CI, not Sally Hen.. Whatever you call her."

Once again Amy just shrugged, "Ok, so he's the one that's into something. Why do you think he'd keep those kinds of records at his office?"

"I don't," Tony replied. "But it'll give us an idea of where to go looking for him at least. Maybe we'll get lucky."

"Not," Amy stressed that word, "a good idea, Tony. In fact, it's got to be one of your biggest turkeys! How do we even get in there? It would take time and I

74

doubt this Eleanor bitch is just going to let us walk right in and turn his computer on."

Unfortunately, Tony had that mischievous smile that he usually reserved for when he wanted to have sex. Amy found it very concerning that she only half wished that was what he had in mind right now. The other half wished she knew why he kept glancing up at the Foo King Junior sign.

Tony waited until they were sitting in the parking lot of the professional building that housed Cashton's offices then, as he hit the dial on his phone, he said, "Haven't you guys heard the news? There's a mad bomber on the loose today." A few seconds later he said, "Hi there, I'm the guy that blew up the Foo King on the L-5. I got even with them and now I'm going to take care of the doctor that pumped my stomach after I ate there. Dr. Herbert Cashton! Death to the corporate, um, booger heads!" Tony hung up.

Amy's eyes had gotten so big they hurt, "They're going to see who called, Tony."

Shannon, who had been eating in the back seat, now leaned over and asked, "Booger heads?"

Tony still looked smug as he pointed to the phone in his hand. He set it down and pulled another phone from his jacket, "This one is mine." He nodded to the one he sat down and had placed the call with, "That's Freddy's phone. I took it from him after we cut him loose."

Shannon almost laughed but was trying too hard to look mad, "You're a dirty fucker. Do you know that?"

Amy pushed her back and then snapped, "And I don't want to hear you say the F word ever again!"

The teenager just shrugged and before taking another bite of her sandwich she said, "How can I not talk about eating a Foo King Burger when I'm eating a Foo King Burger!"

"Relax," Tony said ignoring the kid. "Freddy's got an alibi. He lost his phone, remember?"

Amy's head dropped against the steering wheel, "And if Summer's boys pick him up, he's going to rat you out, Tony."

"And tell them what?" Tony snickered. "That I took it from him in a house he was breaking in…" Tony pointed to the front door of the building where a horde of panicked people were rushing for their cars. He doubted if any of them believed there was a real bomb. More than likely they all wanted to get out of here before the all clear sounded and their bosses made them go back to work.

"Stay in the car," said Shannon as she watched the two Colonial Agents get out. They did not even bother to tell her she was right. When the doors slammed, Shannon just mumbled with a half-eaten burger in her mouth, "Assholes. It's a doctor's office. What could possibly happen here?"

As they walked against the tide of humanity towards a side door, Amy just asked, "Ok, genius. This is your idea. What's the plan?"

Tony pulled out his badge and then held the fire door open as people rushed out. He yelled to them as they did, "Colonial Fire and Rescue! We have confirmed there is a bomb in this building. Please exit the entire property as you…" A lull in the traffic stopped Tony's spiel and he just walked on inside. Amy closed the door behind them and dropped a locking pin in the mechanism so that nobody could follow them.

A few more people came down the fire stairs and Tony turned them around with his badge and an excuse of, "This way is blocked, main entrance please!" When the coast was clear he asked Amy, "Three-oh-two, right? I hope that really is on the third floor." She did not bother to answer the obviously ridiculous question. Amy just took the lead and was amazed that this plan was really working. They saw no one until they reached the very bland looking door that had three-oh-two on it.

The door had been left open, but as Amy found, was blocked by a woman heading in the opposite direction. This plump looking middle-aged woman in a business suit had her hands full of papers and notebooks. The woman looked nervous and then she became quite demanding when she said, "Who are you?"

Amy gulped and was not so sure if it was a good idea to speak. She might have been using a thick accent on the phone but realized that this woman, that sounded very much like Eleanor, might recognize her voice anyway. Fortunately, Tony stepped up and waived his badge, "There's a bomb in the building ma'am. I'm sorry, but I'm afraid I can't let you take anything with you. It could be the bomb."

The woman almost became cross-eyed when she replied, "These are notebooks. I don't think they'll go boom."

Tony began dog paddling at the woman's papers until they were all over the floor. Then he led her to the elevator and pushed her in. She was protesting the entire way, "You're supposed to take the stairs!"

"Not in an emergency, ma'am," Tony told her as the doors closed. "The elevator is faster. Trust me, I'm a fireman!" He then ran back down to the office and closed the door behind him. He locked it just to be safe. Then Tony put his hands on his hips and looked down at Amy who was shuffling around the papers on the floor. He asked, "Anything good besides the shot of your ass I'm getting right now?"

Amy threw one of the notebooks at him. She slung it a little harder than she might should have, but Tony caught it anyway. He thumbed through it, "Appointments book." He shoved it in his pocket and then headed for the back part of the office, "I'll check their computers." He came back out a second later, "There are no computers!"

Amy was about finished with her sweep, so she looked up at him and grumbled, "File cabinets, dumb ass!"

Tony got a strange look on his face, "What's a file cabinet?"

Now, Amy was really grumbling as she got up. She grabbed him by the ear and pulled him back to what looked like a file room. She explained, "A lot of businesses with clients that like privacy don't use computers. They're too easy to hack into."

Tony was amazed at the shelf after shelf of paper he was looking at. His jaw about dropped and then he asked, "How many dead trees did it take to stock this room?"

Amy pushed him back in the hallway and commanded, "Go check the doctor's desk. I'll glance through here." Unfortunately, even if Amy would not admit it, she had no idea where to even start. As she glared in amazement at all the manila folders she finally realized where to go - the K section. She thumbed through the names until she reached Kingsley. Sure enough, there was a folder for

Myra, but Amy already figured that. There was one other file with that last name, so Amy yanked it and to her surprise Eleanor had been telling the truth. The file wasn't for Tasha, or even Natasha. It was a file on Roy Kingsley!

Amy browsed through the file and realized she did not understand most of it. What was clear though, was that Cashton had done some kind of procedure on Roy and the dates were even recent. The last check was just yesterday! Amy mumbled to herself, "This doesn't make any sense."

"Amy, get in here!" She did just as Tony had asked and found him in Cashton's office. Unlike most of the rest of the office he did have a computer screen sitting on his desk. What Tony showed her on it was nothing that Amy had expected to see. It was a news stream with that woman reporter. Roy Kingsley's face was in a little window beside the live report that appeared to be coming from downtown at the police station.

"Again," the reporter said, "this is Jessica Walsh, and police officials are now officially confirming that one of the dead from this morning's explosion was none other than Roy Kingsley, son of prominent businessman, Hyrum Kingsley."

Amy slapped the folder down on the desk and added to the reporter's statement, "And patient of one Dr. Herbert Cashton." Amy sighed, leaned her neck forward, and rubbed her temples, "This day just keeps getting better."

Tony's phone went off and he almost ignored it as he had been doing most of the day now. When he looked at his screen, he had expected to see Calvin's name but was a little ticked to see Shannon's instead. Tony answered, "We told you to stay in the car!"

"I am in the car, jackass," the teenager replied with a biting tone. Before Tony could reply she added, "You got about a half dozen firemen headed your way, only I don't think they're firemen."

"What do you mean?" Tony was confused. "If they look like firemen then why don't you think they are?"

"Because they're all carrying machineguns!"

Tony hung up without so much as another word. He looked at Amy and growled, "You just had to say it, didn't you?"

"What?" Amy was still confused as he grabbed her by the arm, and they fled to the hallway.

They came out of nowhere and despite the fact that they were at least half dressed as firemen, Tony was pretty sure they did not work for his uncle. Instead of axes, picks, and other assorted firemen stuff, these guys were armed to the teeth. They did have on the gas masks that firemen typically wore but they were not of the right make to be city issue. Only someone who knew anything about the fire department would probably notice that.

One of them made a certain swinging motion with his arm, and while Tony did not see it clearly, only out of the corner of his eye, he could guess what the guy was doing. That left Tony just enough time to do the only thing he could think of. He pushed Amy back in the office door and then the world turned blank, his ears began to ring, and Tony was pretty sure he was dying.

Chapter 17

It was really hard to make out what this new guy was thinking. Cal found himself infuriated as he stood there and watched Tasha Kingsley, from behind a two-way mirror, give a statement to a couple of cops and a court reporter. Jake Barton, on the other hand, showed no visible emotion at all. He just watched, obviously hanging on every word, but never even so much as flinching no matter what the woman said.

Cal thought it was interesting how Kingsley had her lawyer present. Wasn't she supposed to be the victim here? What did a victim need with an attorney? It was just one more straw on his back and he was afraid the next one might break it. When one of the cops held up a picture of Norman Scoggins, Tasha quickly nodded in the affirmative and said in no uncertain terms, "That's him, officer."

No one in the interview room seemed to notice when people behind the mirror talked. It was obviously sound-proofed well enough, so Cal spoke up to the little gathering around him, "That's ridiculous. You can't just show her one picture. That's leading the witness or," Cal thought about it and capped his own statement with, "something."

Hal Summers, quite contrary to what Cal expected, did not blow up. He simply looked Calvin's way and smiled as he replied, "She saw what she saw, Brandt. Can't change that."

Cal huffed and then nudged Jake as he said, "You're not going to let them get away with this, are you?"

"Shut up and listen," was the only thing Jake had to say to that. He was not mean about it. In fact, for Calvin, the guy almost sounded a little too cool. Cal was now starting to rethink his earlier admiration of this former Green Beret.

When the interview finally ended, Kingsley and her lawyer both smiled and thanked the officers before leaving. The light then came on in the observation room and it was Gary Moss who spoke up first, "I think, due to the current situation, we might should put off you presenting your credentials for at least a week, Major."

"Do what you want to do, Moss," Jake told him. "I already got dinner plans for tonight. I'm not changing them."

Another cop knocked on the door and when he got permission to enter, he came in, whispered something to Summers, and then left promptly. Everyone looked to the chief of police who waved it off as, "Another bomb threat. We've been getting them all day, ever since Norm torched ole Roy Boy this morning."

"How many?" Jake asked the man.

Summers just shrugged and said, "I don't know, maybe six or seven. They're nothing to worry about. No more bombs have gone off."

Jake held his cool, "Well, I hope that doesn't mean you're not going to check them out."

"Hey, look here Mister Treaty Guy," Summers obviously took offense. He was a burly fellow and Jake figured the man was probably used to getting his way by bowing-up like a gorilla. Jake just silently and coldly let the guy vent, "We don't need you experts from Earth coming here and telling us how to run our colony, ok? We were doing just fine before all you people showed up."

"Yeah, I can see that," Jake replied flatly.

There was no tone of any kind in Jake's voice, let alone an insulting one. Hal Summers chose to take one anyway, "For your information, Mister Deputy, we had a couple of grocery stores, another Foo King, and an empty school that all got threats. The only one that turned out to be close to real was a couple of kids setting off a stink bomb, which was really a waste of time seeing as how they were out of school today anyway."

Jake acted as if he were listening to a serious report. With his even voice he asked, "And this last one?"

"Another wild goose chase," Summers replied. "It was some doctors building way over on the other side of the island. Who would want to blow up a doctors building?"

The same cop, that had delivered the first message, stuck his head in the door again. This time the kid looked excited and had obviously not waited for permission. He was also talking in a high squeak instead of a whisper, "Chief! We're getting multiple reports of gun fire at that doctors office!"

"Wait a minute," Cal said with no small amount of alarm. He looked directly at the young officer and asked, "Is this Dr. Herbert Cashton's office?"

Summers was completely taken by surprise and was just a tad bit confused by the question. He asked Brandt, "The plastic surgeon that does all those celebrities? What's he got to do with anything?"

Jake grabbed his man by the sleeve and led him out the door as he told the head cop, "You got your suspect, Chief. Unless I miss my guess, you'll have your hands full with that for the time being."

Summers, thankfully, took the bait. He laughed at the Deputy Marshall and boasted, "Oh, we'll catch Scoggins. Just you wait and see. I always was a better cop than him."

Before closing the door to the room, Jake looked back at the guy and said, "Yeah, I can see that." Then, after a second of thinking on the matter, Jake turned back completely and said, "I'll bet you a hundred marks you can't catch him before night fall."

Summers eyes narrowed and he said, "You're on!"

They reached the back door of the station and stopped there. It was relatively private, so Jake told his red-faced subordinate, "Ok, get it off your chest."

Cal fired up, "How could you do that? You're making a bet about the life of a friend of mine. Do you really think they're going to bring him in? If Hyrum Kingsley thinks he killed Roy, then..."

Jake cut in, "Then he won't do anything else that they wouldn't already do. At least this way Summers is going to want to get him back here before they put a hole in his head. It also keeps the city police busy and off of our backs."

That did nothing to relieve Cal's anger, but he was having a hard time finding any logical fault with Jake's argument. Cal almost hit the wall with his fist, but Jake told him, "Save it, Agent. We're going to need it before this day is over with. I just got a feeling about that."

"It's not easy," Cal replied. His face was still red, but his voice became a bit more tempered when he said, "How could you just, just, callously take all of that?"

"Really?" Jake asked. "And how is it you went and told everybody in that room the name of our best lead? What those bozos in there think about your buddy isn't going to change no matter what we say. So, let them have their fun and lets us concentrate on something a little more important, all right, agent?"

Jake held up a slip of paper that had the address of the doctor's office on it, "I took this from that kid at the door when we walked by. I got a feeling this is where we'll find all our lost sheep but..."

Cal took the paper and read the address. Then he saw the name of the guy who called it in, "I hope they didn't take this name seriously. Seymour Butts?"

"Is that Cashton's office?" It was all Jake cared about at the moment.

"I'll have to look at my notebook in the car, but," Cal nodded a little, "yeah, it looks like the right address."

Jake snatched the note back and then said in a stern and commanding voice, "Good. This isn't all we're going to have to do though. I need you to call back to the station. I got another detail for your crew."

Chapter 18

The knock at the door was enough to send shivers up her spine. At least this guy was always polite enough to say who he was shortly after that. "Are you all right, my dear? May I enter?"

She deflated in relief as she walked over to the door and opened it. He was polite like that. He always waited for her to open the door and never came right in, even if she said to. Sally had no idea why that was the case. As near as she could tell there was not a single door in this entire building that had a lock on it. It was one more curious thing about this place, but all the rest put together was not as curious as the guy who ran it. How did a guy with the last name of Solomon end up with a first name like Enrique?

He was an older man with a graying beard, and he wore robes that made him look more like a Catholic monk than a Jewish Rabbi. He was always quite polite, and Sally wondered if she bugged him a little too much. Her questions were always the same, "Have you heard anything?"

Enrique always sounded calm and quite reassuring, "I am sure that he will be back soon enough."

"No," Sally said with her head dipped low, "I don't mean him. I mean, you know…"

"I'm sure we'll hear soon enough, my child," the Rabbi told her. He continued, "In the meantime, it might be wise if you got some rest. As I have been told, you had a long night and I know you have not slept a wink since you got here."

Sally sat down on the bed, but she would not lay down. She could not force herself to do it. She tried pushing yet another tear back as she told him, "How can I? I got my best friend in the world shot, maybe even dead. I.. I, god, this whole thing is such a big mess."

The next voice to speak was not that of the Rabbi. It came from Norm and he sounded and moved as if he were in a hurry. He walked right past Enrique and turned on the video monitor in the corner of the room. After he selected the news feed, he stood back so the others could see. They all watched as Chief Summers told an assembled group of reporters, "We believe that this man, Norman Scoggins, was seeking revenge for last night's shooting of another Colonial Agent."

The reporters erupted in a roar of questions. Summers picked Jessica Walsh out of the crowd and answered her question first, "No, we have no proof that Roy Kingsley was in anyway involved in last night's shooting. We just know that he was the victim of a deliberate explosion that killed both him and several bystanders this morning."

Enrique looked to Norm and told him, "I do not believe you or the girl will be safe here any longer."

"Why do you think I came back when I did?" Norm replied. "I heard this on the radio in my car."

Enrique nodded in agreement, "Hal will no doubt think of me first."

Sally was still sniffling on the bed when she asked with some concern, "I don't understand? I.. I thought you said nobody knew about this place."

"Nobody does, Sally," Norm told her. "Only Enrique and I were partners for a lot of years when we worked for the department. Now that he's looking for me, the first thing Hal is going to do is start running down my old acquaintances."

Enrique added, "And it will not take him long to find out where I have been. He had no more love for me than he did Norman."

Norm pulled his phone from his pocket and checked the stopwatch he had running, "He's already got my house staked out. They've probably already questioned Darcy. That means he's going to be sending units to as many addresses as he can locate right off the bat."

Enrique sighed in regret, "And Wallace Young is still in Warrants. He knows what I do and where. As I recall, Norm, he didn't much like you either."

Sally was shaking her head in disbelief, "I don't know if I can take much more of this. I just want to find Herb and vanish. He can get us out. I told you, he's got connections."

In a hurried fashion, Norm went to the closet and began pulling out his gear. As he did, he told Sally, "Unless I miss my guess, your doctor buddy is long gone." Norm tossed out his high threat level body armor onto the bed. Then he started pulling a few weapons out of the bag that was still in the closet. He asked Enrique,

"Put the rest of these back where I had them when we're gone, ok?" Then Norm said to Sally, "Don't worry. This is almost over with. I found the truck."

Sally's eyes got big, "How? Where? I mean... were those men there?"

"Shake enough trees and the rotten apple is gonna fall," Norm told her.

Sally bit her bottom lip. She put a hand on her stomach and thought about what he had just said. She had been too busy running and being scared to think about anything that might happen after this. Now it just occurred to her, "I'm going to jail, aren't I?"

Enrique put a hand on her shoulder, "You did not know anyone was going to be killed. Your intentions in this matter were noble."

Norm was a little less comforting. He saw no reason to lie to the girl, "Natasha played you, Sally. It's that simple. She played all of us."

"I can't believe," Sally fought to hold back more tears. "I mean... I knew her since third grade. I.. I can't believe she'd kill her own husband."

Still the comforter, Enrique told the young girl, "She may not have known."

Sally cried back, "I helped set it up!"

At least some of the truth was good here. After sliding his vest on, Norm slipped his jacket back on over it and then told the girl, "He's right, Sally. All we know for sure is that she tried to set him up. We don't know if she actually pulled the trigger." Norm stuffed some extra magazines in his pockets, "And one thing is absolutely for certain here. That was not a drug shipment in that warehouse. Maybe she didn't know either. Doesn't matter now anyway."

A call sounded and it proved to be Enrique's phone that he had stashed in his robes. He answered, listened, and then told Norm, "They are already here. Do you have a safe place to take the girl?"

"I think so, but," Norm readied his sub-machinegun and then shouldered his other bag, "I'm running short on time if I want to catch these guys."

"Then you must hurry," Enrique fanned them both towards the door, "God go with you, my old friend. I'll stall them at the gate as long as I can."

There was one thing that Norm could never figure out. He could certainly understand how his old friend, one of the toughest bastards he had ever known, could give it all up and become some kind of weird Jewish monk. He could certainly comprehend how what started out as the shooting of one of his best friends could be spun around and twisted to look like it was his fault. What he could not quite figure out was how a girl, that was not quite half his age, could not even keep up with him as he ran with a hundred pounds of gear strapped to his body.

They had not even made it halfway to his planned escape route when Sally had fallen hopelessly behind. Norm had to stop and go back for the girl who was bent over and gasping for air. He had to grab her by the arm and drag her along. She even protested, "I'll stay, they don't want me."

"Enough people want you out of the way, girl," Norm told her as he pulled Sally into one of the many gardens on the property. He realized now that she was slowing him down to a trot. "You wouldn't be safe with the cops. You'd wind up dead, or worse, sooner or later."

"Worse than dead?" That thought bounced around in Sally's brain until she suddenly found herself looking at a brick wall that by all appearances belonged to the one that ran the length of the property. Then Norm pulled at a bush that turned out to be a handle for a trap door. Sally was not so sure she wanted to crawl down into the tunnel beneath it. The place looked dirty!

Norm gestured for her to follow him, but at first, she hesitated. He could guess why. He even told her it was clean, but then Sally surprised him by asking an intelligent question, "How do you know the cops won't be waiting on the other side? Won't they have surrounded this place or something?"

"It's a big property, Sally," Norm told her. "They'll cover the gates, but unless they know I'm here for sure they won't have the manpower to surround the place. Besides, this leads to another property that nobody knows the monastery owns."

"Oh, geez," Sally then grunted after she got on her knees in the dirt and prepared to crawl in. She wondered what kind of Rabbi Jewish Monks would have an escape tunnel! She asked Norm and he replied, "The paranoid kind." He then pushed her into the tunnel. The only good thing that Sally had to say about the experience was that the tunnel was short. She found herself coming up in what appeared to be the back room of - a laundry? All she knew for certain was that there was a lot of clothing in plastic all hanging on some kind of conveyor belt system. There was also a little Chinese guy waiting on her. He was an even bigger surprise when he helped pull her out of the tunnel with a hand that he then used to shake with, "Sam Goldberg, nice to meet you, Sally."

Norm crawled out of the tunnel with ease and then after a nod to Sam, both men slid a dry press machine back over the tunnel hole. Then Sam asked them, "You guys need a change?"

It was something that Norm had not even considered. He just looked himself over and decided there were no clothes that could hide all of the gear he was handling. He told Sam, "They don't know what we're wearing. I don't think we'll bother."

Sally was busy looking at the dirt on her clothes and all she could say to that was, "Eww!"

"We don't have time," Norm told her definitively. He grabbed Sally and began to pull her through the sea of moving clothes as he asked Sam, "Is it clear?"

Sam followed them as he replied, "Your car is right where you left it. Didn't see any cops." Sam peeled off when they reached the front of the store and sat back down behind his counter. His job was done now, "Good luck, Norm." Once the two fugitives were out of the store he added, "L'Chaim. You're gonna need it."

This particular street was not very heavily trafficked. It was probably why the monastery wanted their dry-cleaning business/escape tunnel here in the first place. There were no official openings to the grounds that led to this street, so as Sam had said, Norm saw no sign of a police presence. He was still not taking any chances as he drug Sally along towards his car. Then he felt her jerk away from his grasp.

That set off all kinds of alarm bells, and suddenly, Norm made sense of all that he had seen. A single man was in the car in front of his, and as the man climbed out, Norm realized he knew guy. It was Ted Hawson who was a well-known heavy for the Texans. Across the street, in the direction that Sally was running, another similar looking car was parked with three men standing around it. Sally was running for one of the men! Suddenly, Norm realized why when he recognized the guy. Norm wanted to go after Sally. He thought about yelling for her to come back, but their time had run out.

The only thing that Norm could think to say when he saw Big Ted draw a weapon was the mumble that crossed his lips, "Hal, you son of a bitch!"

Sally ran into Herb Cashton's arms and hugged him for all that she was worth. He too slipped his arms around her and held on tightly. When Sally heard the first gunshots fired, somewhere over her shoulder, she tried to jerk away. She then realized that Herb would not let go nor would he move from the spot they were standing. She looked up at him and he was smiling. She was confused. Then she saw the syringe in his hand. Then she saw nothing at all.

Chapter 19

Whatever had happened was causing her ears to ring like somebody was banging on a couple of big church bells in her head, but Amy found that she could still think and move. She saw Tony stumble back in the door and then fall over a couch. She was not sure exactly what happened, but then it did not take a rocket scientist to figure out that they were under attack. She had landed on the floor, so she stayed there as she rolled back over to the door, pulled her weapon, and began firing through the smoke that was now choking the hallway.

There was a scream, followed by some frantic shouts. Amy took that as a good sign that she had hit something. It only added to the sensation that was working her body and now she felt like she wanted to throw up. The smoke was bad enough, but this had to be the first time that Amy had ever fired her gun at anything but a paper target. Her hand started to shake as the shouts began to die down. Then a horde of bullets began impacting around her and now her hands were really shaking.

Amy rolled back out of the doorway no sooner than the debris of plaster and wood stopped falling. She crawled over to Tony who was still rolling around the floor with his hands covering his eyes. She steadied him and then tried to pull his hands away. He screamed at her, "I can't see!"

There were new sounds outside the door. Amy could not exactly make out what was going on, but there was yelling and movement. Then another volley of fire began tearing up the wall around the door. She gulped when she realized that, had she still been there, she would probably be dead now. They were shooting much lower this time.

Tony was still covering his eyes when he leaned up, but he sounded more in control of himself as he yelled over the sounds of gunfire, "They're trying to flank us."

"How?!" Amy had never really used terms such as 'flank.' Now with her life hanging in the balance, Amy could figure out the implications. They were trying to go around them only, how did you do that in an office building?

Tony, still squirming an in pain, told her, "The wall over by the records room."

Amy left him and ran for the room where they did their day surgery. She quickly found what she was looking for and wheeled it into the records room. She laid it flat and then retreated back to one side of the open door. Sure enough, and not nearly long enough for Amy's tastes, a wall of plaster and cheap metal came flying out of the room in a lethal wave of debris. Amy was still coughing as she peeked back in the room and saw the men with automatic weapons rushing in. One of them spotted her and prepared to fire. He only stopped when he realized what he was standing over.

Taking as much cover as she could, Amy began to empty the magazine of her weapon. She probably did not have many rounds left when a bullet struck one of the two oxygen tanks she had left in the floor. It made a loud whistle that sounded closer to a shuttle engine at this range. The heat from the bullet and the sparks from metal on metal then ignited the expanding cloud of pure oxygen. Amy was actually surprised at the sound that the explosion made. It was more like very loud 'crump' than a proper bang.

When she looked back in the room, Amy could no longer hold the contents of her stomach. The smells of burned paper, flesh, and the dust of plaster all mixed with the sights of those charred bodies. It was too much. She was still heaving on her knees when she felt the hand on her shoulder. Amy almost shot Tony at that point. He was stumbling and his eyes were puffy, but they were open a little bit.

When Amy got to her feet, she found out that she was almost as bad as Tony on the stumbling thing. She fell back against the wall and then took a very deep breath. Tony was still rubbing at his eyes and then he looked back into what used to be the records room to make sure his first glance had been right. The flash, that had set the now growing fire, had been so strong that even he could make it out in the waiting room with his eyes closed and hands over them.

"What the hell did you do?" Tony asked in a very demanding tone.

That was enough for Amy. She had no wish to look back at the carnage she had just made. She had gathered enough of her strength and wits to take Tony's arm over her shoulder and lead him away. She also did not bother to answer his question. When she got him back in the waiting room, he pointed at the chewed-up door and said, "We need to get out of here. They're falling back."

Amy was both frightened and surprised, "Because of what I did?"

"No offense, babe," Tony told her, "but I don't think so."

As they passed by one of the windows, Amy looked down in the parking lot and saw the armored vehicles of the Wehrmacht, coming up the nearby street. Of course, it was obvious that they would not get here in time to trap the heavily armed firemen. Those guys had gotten down the stairs even faster than they came up them and were already loading up in their van.

Amy moaned, "Oh great! Saved from sadistic psychopathic murderers by a bunch of Nazi goons. A girl's dream come true." She wasted no more time and helped Tony down the stairway they had come up. The Germans were already surrounding the building when she got him back to her car and helped him sit on the hood. Tony held up one hand signaling Amy that he needed no more help and was rubbing his eyes with the other. He probably did not see the Germans that came up and pointed weapons at them, but there was no doubt to Amy that he heard them yelling.

Raising her hands in surrender, Amy told the three soldiers, "Um spreken.. Whatever the hell you say, don't shoot?!"

Horst came strolling up in time to hear Amy's tirade. He tapped one of his men on the shoulder and sent his grenadiers away. Then he smiled at the two Colonial Agents, "Well, I see you two are not having much luck today. You seem to keep showing up at all the wrong places."

Tony squinted at the guy, "Oh, don't hand me that crap, Horst. You followed us here."

Horst simply smiled, tipped his hat, and said as he left, "I will have one of my medics have a look at your eyes, Mr. Tippet. Good day."

Amy waited for the man to get far enough away before she asked Tony, "What the hell is that guy after?"

"I don't know," Tony admitted in a tone that sounded out how much pain he was in. "Whatever it is, he owes us one."

Since Tony was trying to stand back up, Amy helped him and replied as she did, "The only problem is, he probably thinks he repaid the favor by not shooting us." It was only then, struggling to help a resistant Tony, that Amy actually paid attention to the car. She almost dropped him as she ran to the back door and opened it. That left Tony struggling to catch up. When he was steadied on the open back door he looked in and thought he could make out a half-eaten hamburger that was now slung from one side of the backseat to the other.

Amy gulped in a panicked frenzy, "Where the hell is Shannon?"

Tony huffed, "Barbara's going to kill us."

Chapter 20

It hurt going on, but Tony had to admit the solution that the German medic was applying around his eyes was working. His vision was clearing up. The fuzzy shape that had just stopped in front of him started to take on more details until it formed into the image of a very angry looking new guy boss man. Tony was starting to wonder if it was too late for the medic to give him something else to make things fuzzy again. He gulped and then said, "Um, hi?"

Jake held his look of anger and made sure that Amy, who was sitting in the back hatch of the armored personnel carrier with Tony, got her share of it too. Then Jake told the medic to take a hike before asking, "So what did you two geniuses find out by blowing up an office building?"

Amy pointed back to the building, that had smoke coming out of its top windows now, and meekly said, "That's not really our fault."

Calvin, who was standing next to Jake, was a bit more sympathetic, "You two ok?"

Tony nodded as he sniffled and kept from trying to rub his eyes. He had his own angry look when he finally managed to glance up at Jake again. Then he said, "Look Mister Deputy Marshal. No offense but we don't know you from Adam."

Calvin tried to intervene, but Jake stopped him and said, "It's ok. He's right about that much." Then even the pretense of civility evaporated as Jake turned his attention back to Tony, "So that gives you the excuse to go off playing detective and not even bothering to tell anybody?" Once more Jake commented back to Calvin, "I take back what I said earlier. What this department needs more than new gear is some," he raised his voice to a sharp rebuke and looked to Tony when he finished his statement with, "ADULTS."

Amy meekly raised a finger and volunteered in an almost submissive way, "We know Danni's shooting and the bombing from this morning are connected."

Jake now fixed his gaze on her and it caused Amy to retreat back in an invisible shell. She acted almost like he was going to hit her as he said, "And you found out that this Dr. Cashton was Danni's CI. That he and Sally what's her name helped this Tasha Kingsley woman kill her husband Roy. That they were the ones that brought in Danni and probably set her and Norm up, too."

Tony was still trying very hard to keep his hands away from his eyes as he responded, "That sums it up pretty good."

Amy was still being very meek as she asked, "How did you guys figure that out?"

"Very carefully," Jake told her sternly. He also added, "That and a lot more. Oh and, by the way, we didn't have to blow up an office building in the process!"

"Really," Amy was almost pleading, "that wasn't our fault, well, not mostly." Then she spit out as rapidly as she could, "But we lost Shannon and I think she might have been kidnapped."

Cal's jaw dropped, "You had Shannon with you? In the middle of an office bombing?!"

"Actually," Tony closed his eyes and raised his hand, "it was a fire fight, not an office bombing. I called in the bomb threat."

Amy drew up and whispered, "Yeah, that part was kind of our fault."

Cal broke out into a very frantic panic, "Barbara is going to kill all of us!"

Jake had to wonder about this woman that he had even yet to meet. He summoned some calm and told Cal, "No, not everybody. I won't let her do that, just these two." Then he looked back at the two rogue agents and asked, "So, do you have any idea where the kid is?" When neither answered he asked them, "Did you do something as basic as try and call her? Maybe she's hiding out around here. First rule of a missing person's case is make sure the person is actually missing."

"Oh my god," Amy suddenly brightened up, "I put my phone on silent when we went in the building." She quickly grabbed her phone from her pocket and was astonished at what she saw.

Cal saw the look and suddenly felt some hope, "Did she call you?"

"Um," Amy tried to look calm and collected, although she was sure she was doing a bad job of it. "No, she sent us a text."

Jake asked in a matter of fact tone, "What does it say?"

"Well," Amy licked her lips and forced a smile, "the good news is she wasn't kidnapped."

Calvin's eyes widened, "And the bad? There is a bad, right, Amy?"

Amy tilted her head back and forth in a perky manner before spitting it out, "She's hiding in the van with the people who just tried to kill us." Amy then shrugged as she looked up at Calvin and Jake, "So, it's not really our fault, right? I did tell her to stay in the car."

As Calvin went back to panicking, Jake stayed cool and asked a more relevant question, "Does she know where she's at?"

Amy got very defensive as she thrust the phone at Jake, "You read it! That's all she said, OK!?"

"Fortunately for you, Agent Hiller," Jake responded to the girl, "I got a pretty good idea of where they're going." He then nodded to Calvin, who then stopped his panicked frenzy and dialed up his own phone. Cal looked somewhat relieved when he finished the call and told Jake, "I think we got 'em this time."

"Tell Alvarez and Johnson," Jake commanded, "to watch for this van. If it shows up, we'll be there in," Jake realized he had no idea how long it would take for them to get there, "however long it takes." As Calvin did just that, Jake looked to his other two agents and told them, "And you two can go back to the station and wait for your spankings."

"No way," Tony said as he stood up. He forced his hands to stay by his side as he told the American, "This is our family, not yours. We're going too."

"Agent Tippet," Jake responded to that, "you just had a concussion grenade go off in your face. You're not going to be any use to anybody and probably a danger to us and yourself. You were certainly that even before the grenade."

"How are you going to stop me?" Tony just shrugged, "I'm already in hot water. How much more trouble can I get in?"

Jake was satisfied with the answer he got so, "You two follow us, and this time, make sure the Germans aren't following you."

Amy was stunned as she watched Jake and Cal walk back to their car. She grabbed Tony's arm and asked, "How did he know that?"

"Lucky guess," was all Tony could figure. He tried to take a step but almost stumbled. Amy kept him from falling completely over. After she got him back up straight, she made sure she gave him a kiss that left him a little stunned. Tony even had to ask, "What was that for?"

Amy took a breath and could not look him in the face as she said, "Saving my life back there."

Tony was not even sure he had done that. He let it go. He liked kissing this girl, so he did it again.

Chapter 21

All in all, Shannon was kind of wishing she had not been playing the video game when Amy and Tony decided to crash the doctors building. She might have noticed what the 'firemen' had driven up in. She had only caught sight of them when they were rushing in the building. Shannon might not have even thought to warn her friends had it not been for all the machineguns these guys were packing. She might have also thought to look for more of these guys, or at least seen the two who were sweeping through the parking lot. Not only were they heavily armed, but one of them had his phone in hand and it was plugged in to some weird looking antenna that was clipped to his fake fireman's coat. Somehow, that thing had led them right to Amy's car.

The only good news was that Shannon had seen them long before they saw her. She beat a hasty retreat out of the far side of the vehicle, staying as low as she could. She watched from behind a nearby vehicle as the two firemen moved in on Amy's vehicle with their weapons raised. They were not satisfied with what they found and this left Shannon having to form yet another plan, and quickly, because they began searching in her direction. This time the guy with the crazy antenna was eyes only and it made escape all that much harder.

Shannon used the only advantage she could figure. They had not seen her yet and there was always the possibility that they might not even be sure that she really even existed. The teenager crawled around some vehicles until she saw the feet of the one of the firemen stop. Then she saw his knee hit the pavement and that sent Shannon rolling up into a ball behind a tire. The other guy was still moving, and she had to think of something quick or he was going to see her!

Then Shannon formulated another new plan. She got up from behind the tire and ran for the nearest by-standers. The fireman began to pursue until Shannon ran up to the nearest by-stander, some plump woman in a business suit, and Shannon wrapped her arms around the woman in a big hug. Shannon also made sure she loudly screamed, "MOMMY!"

When Shannon peeked out from the embrace that she had on the confused woman, she saw that the fireman guy stopped running in her direction and then went back to searching. Then Shannon told the confused woman, "Can you help me find my mommy, please?"

"Um," the woman was still confused, but she softened and told Shannon, "Of course, dear. I'm Eleanor and I will gladly help you find your mommy." At that point, with the fireman now looking in another direction, Shannon let go and ran off with a, "Thanks, lady!"

Shannon stopped next to the white cargo van that was just sitting, open, by the building. The nearest fireman was at the front door, but he did not seem to be looking for her. Then Shannon took out the electric car key she had lifted out of Eleanor's pocket. She was not sure which car it belonged to, but it should make a sound when she hit the button. Unfortunately, the sound of an explosion and falling glass had muffled the beeping noise of whatever car had made it. The sight of firemen, including the ones that had been looking for her, rushing in Shannon's direction was enough of an incentive for her to give up on hiding in another car. She had one option left and that was the van she was behind.

The good news turned out to be that it was full of pallets and crates. They were easily opened, and Shannon ducked into one that proved to be half filled with little bags of white powder. Shannon did not need to be an adult to figure out what they were. She closed the crate behind her, content that she was safe enough for now. Then the bad news became clear when she heard a multitude of men jumping in the back of the van and closing its roll-down door. She heard them yelling at each other, "Come on, man! The damn Krauts are almost here!"

One particular guy seemed to be taking charge. Shannon wanted to peek out of the crate and get a look at him, but when she tried a horde of fireman coats began landing on the crate she was in. The vehicle was also moving now, and she did the only thing she could think of. She sent Amy a text. She wanted to scream when she got no answer and then felt a sigh of relief. She realized the damn volume was still on! Shannon quickly put it on silent and watched the screen in anticipation of some reply. When it finally came, Shannon had not even started reading it when she felt the van come to a halt, heard the back door opening and men jumping out.

Shannon began to breathe a little easier. Then she read the text, "KEEP HEAD DOWN, WE R CUMIN, STAY SAFE, LOVE AMY."

Well that did sound easy enough. Shannon figured she was good to go in the crate, but she did wonder how it was they even knew where to go! If she had to wait on Tony and Amy to figure it out, that could take a little while. Unfortunately, Shannon realized, she did not even know where she was. She could not see crap from inside the crate! Now she was wondering if, just maybe, she should have been interested when her Mom was bitching about the government being too cheap to spring for some standard GPS satellites! If they had then Shannon might have been able to let someone know where she was.

The teenager got a handle on things. She was safe enough for now. She was sitting on a good sum of a very expensive product, which meant the guys who owned it were not likely to dump her crate in a trash compactor or anything melodramatic like that. Since she was in a van, and the stuff was in a crate, they were not likely to open it right now. All she had to do was wait! How hard was that?

The crate shook violently. Shannon almost screamed. Then it shook again, and she felt it jerk upwards. Now it was moving, and she had visions of the damn thing on a conveyor belt headed for a big fire! Then she dropped without any warning and this time Shannon could not help the yelp. She was gritting her teeth as she watched the crate door come open. She had to shield her eyes from the light that was only being blocked out by a couple of dark blobs standing in front of the source. Shannon heard what she was sure was the bolt of a gun being cocked.

With a forced smile she told the blobs, "Anybody order pizza?" Shannon had been pretty sure the ruse wouldn't work. She was right yet again.

Chapter 22

The hazy darkness began shaping itself into blobs of darkness that were dancing around in front of the light. It took Sally's mind a minute to realize that while the images in front of her did not make any sense, they were somehow real. Then, as her mind chewed on that, a frightened thought struck her. She had somehow passed out! Quickly, she began to frantically search through her memories to make sense out of what happened. Had that really been Herb that she ran to? Right now, that seemed more like a dream.

Sally let the name slip her lips, "Herb?"

To her surprise, the blob in front of her answered and in Herb's voice too! "It's going to be all right, Sally. You're safe now." She then heard him say the strangest thing, "She's waking up. Go tell her I'll be ready in a minute." The voice became stern when it said, "Now! You steroid laced goon!"

It was only when another voice said something that Sally could not make out, that she realized this was not a dream. She then began to realize that neither was Herb Cashton. She really had run to him on the street and he really did... Her eyes flew wide open and the world came into focus, "What's going on?"

Herb put a finger to his lip and tried to calm her down, "You're going to be safe, Sally. Don't worry. I got you away from that psycho, Scoggins. I already have the tickets. We're getting on the first starship off of this rock."

Sally breathed a sigh of relief, "Thank God. I had thought… well I don't know what I thought."

"First though," Herb told her as he took a quick peek over his shoulder, "We have to pick up that errand I sent you on. You know the one, to J&R? You did do that didn't you?"

What the hell did that have to do with anything? Sally began to notice her surroundings now. She was laying in the back seat of a car with Herb nervously twitching over her. All she saw past that through the back window, were rafters and a little day light sneaking past a sheet metal roof. She met Herb's eyes. They were those gentle and loving orbs that she had come to know and trust. She nodded, "Yeah. Just like you told me to."

Herb smiled genuinely and warm. Sally wanted to hug him again, but now he did something with his hands that made a tearing noise, and then he slapped a piece of duct tape over her mouth. The middle-aged doctor snatched her, quite violently, out of the car and then handed her over to a couple of guys wearing suits and cowboy hats.

Then Sally got an even bigger surprise when Tasha stepped up and put a finger to Sally's cheek. Then the woman told one of the two suited goons, "Baxter, you know what to do with her."

The guy promptly and coldly said, "Yes, ma'am."

Tasha giggled as they led the young woman off. She called out to Sally, "No hard feelings, Sal! It's just business."

Herb felt a little uncomfortable. He began pulling at his shirt as he told the dark-headed girl, "You didn't have to like it so much."

Tasha developed a sour face and rolled her eyes at him, "Do you have any idea how long I've wanted to pay that bitch back? It was just icing on the cake that she got to drag Nguyen in on this too."

"Oh god, Tasha," Herb complained. "That was in high school for god's sake.

You can't let anything go, can you?"

Very serious like, Tasha told him, "You remember that, Herb. I didn't tell you to go and screw that little bitch, remember that too." As she led him forward, she also let him know, "Just remember what happened to Roy."

Herb then replied in a very serious way. He knew Tasha would not get the full meaning of it, "Oh believe me. I haven't." Both of them stopped in front of the crew that made up their business partners. They had already slipped on the coveralls for some delivery company and were making ready to leave. Herb was a bit concerned by the extra company they seemed to have acquired on the little errand that had delayed their arrival. He pointed to the young girl and said, "Who the hell is this?"

One of the guys, who was standing next to the teenager, was busy looking at a phone. Herb assumed it was the girl's phone and that was only confirmed when the guy asked the teenager, "What's the password, kid?"

The little teen glibly replied with crossed arms, "Fuck you."

The man promptly pulled a pistol from his shoulder holster and put the barrel on top of the little girl's head, "I'm not playing here, you little shit."

This time the girl was not so defiant as she said, "Neither am I. That's the password."

The man typed it in the phone and seemed satisfied enough as he started reading the screen. Then a moment later he looked to the head man and said, "She's with them screw balls the Krauts have been tailing."

Shannon sneered, "They're cops and they're going to kick your ass when they get here."

The guy laughed at that and then told his boss, "No, seriously, they are on the way though." The head guy seemed a little alarmed by that even as his subordinate pointed out, "What's the problem? We can handle them. If the Krauts hadn't showed up, we already would have."

"Just do what you're told," the head man snapped. He then walked up to Tasha and Herb. He smiled at them and told them, "We're taking off. All that's left is to dispose of the witnesses."

Tasha was confused, "We brought you the last witness already."

The guy that was standing next to Shannon called out, "What do we do with this one?"

"Put her with the other one," the head man replied. He then took a good look at Herb and Tasha. The guy could tell that the fashion model just did not get it. The doctor was a bit smarter though. The way Cashton sweated, the nervous twitch, all told the head guy what to do next. Cashton was about to say something when the head man pulled out his gun. He never got to beg, which was for the best since it was a loathsome practice to the guy who put the bullet in his head.

Then he turned his attention to the screaming Tasha and smiled. He hesitated a moment and then told her, "And the bad part of this is, if you hadn't stolen from our stash, I might have let you live."

"No," Tasha pleaded. "You don't understand! I had to make it look like Roy was…" When it was clear that it was not working. Tasha looked back for her own security. She was shocked to see that they were all dead and laying on the floor. The only one still living was Baxter. He was wiping a knife blade clean. He nodded to the head man. The head man nodded back.

Baxter put away his knife and pulled out a gun. He smiled and said to Tasha, "You have no idea how long I've been waiting to do this. Sorry Mrs. K, but it's just business." He shot her between the eyes.

The head man holstered his weapon. Baxter did the same as he picked up the bag next to him and took it to the head guy. After handing it over, the bag was then quickly handed to yet another jump-suited killer. That guy told both men, "The Oh-Pee just called in. They're definitely on the way. They'll be here in about twenty minutes."

The head man looked to Baxter, "What's the timer set for?"

"It's a standard charge," Baxter replied. "And you have no idea how many strings I had to pull in order to get that."

"You know what to do with it," the head man told his guy before sending him off to take care of one final bit of business before they evacuated. Then he squared off with Baxter.

The alleged bodyguard only just smirked and told him, "Plan on shooting me, too?"

The head man broke out in a laugh and slapped the guy on the arm, "Might be too much trouble."

Baxter did not find anything funny, "That's good. Cause you might need me around to clean-up another one of your messes. My employers will not be very happy when I tell them about all of this."

Now the head man just winked, "We got it under control."

The door to the warehouse's loading dock began to open and the place began to fill with light. A single figure walked in with the sun to his back. Baxter grumbled, "You were saying?"

The head man became a bit concerned and even looked at his watch. They couldn't be anywhere near here yet!

The man at the door raised a grenade launcher to his shoulder and told everyone in the warehouse, "Well I guess we don't have much left to say, do we? So, let's skip that part."

Norm fired.

Chapter 23

The Texans back at the laundry had not been that big of a problem. Norm just wished he had not used his last concussion grenade on them. Like typical bullies they had charged right into the alley after him. They never gave any thought to things like tactics. Norm could have gunned them all down easily, but what the Texian Legion was very good at was holding grudges when you capped one of their guys. That's why Norm left them rolling in the muck of the alley in pain. He also kicked Big Ted in the balls for good measure. The guy had chipped the paint on Norm's car once. Well, Texans weren't the only ones that could hold a grudge.

Norm also did not bother following the vehicle that Sally had been taken away in. He already had a good idea about where it was heading. As it turned out, he was exactly right. They went to the warehouse for a defunct trucking company, once operated by the Texans, and the current location of the moving van that Norm and Danni had seen last night.

The place had been easy enough to find. Norm tailed the bodyguard, Baxter, from the Kingsley estate not long after he paid Hyrum a call. It only made sense that, somehow the Texans were involved since it was hard to move anything substantial, and usually illegal, without their consent. The single biggest mystery was how it got Roy vaporized, and the only answer that Norm could reach was, he must have found out what it was they were really moving. Norm still had no idea what that was. The only way to find out was take these guys down. Now that they had Sally, he had little choice in when to move. It had to be now.

The first salvo came from Norm's grenade launcher, which he discarded on his way to cover. He had no more use for it since he used his last round. Now, Norm figured, he was paying the price for having forgotten to buy the fireworks on Family Day last year. Because of that, Tony and Garcia had almost run through his entire supply of forty-millimeter grenades that they spent most of the night shooting at the buoy out by the station.

Fortunately, the one grenade that Norm had left could do the job he wanted. The guys in the jumpsuits dove for cover when he fired it, but it didn't do them much good. The grenade did not hit the ground and just go off. In fact, it never even hit the ground at all. It sailed through the air, the casing flying off as it did, and then spread its small payload of mini bombs across the arc of its flight. They went off just about at head level and sprayed everything beneath them in a shower of lethal pins that ripped through flesh about as efficiently as a steak knife through butter. Norm could tell it worked because he managed to empty a magazine on his machinegun, and take down three targets, before they even started returning fire.

That was when things got a little more complicated. At first, even the return fire was wild, sporadic, and very light when you considered the hardware these guys were packing. Norm moved from cover to cover and concentrated on the few guys who were shooting at him. He finally ran dry of ammunition for the machinegun and tossed it as he slid beneath the customs van. He pulled the two pistols from the holsters on his hips and then slid to the side of the van where he could find more things to shoot at.

That's when he heard the beating that was coming from inside the van. Then he heard a voice that he recognized, and it was screaming for all it was worth, "HELP!"

Norm's hairs raised and he yelled back, "Shannon?" He then mumbled to himself, "Shit, Barbara's gonna kill me."

The other side was starting to change tactics on Norm. It was no sooner than he realized who was yelling at him from inside the van, when a new volley of fire came flying his way. The weapon making this fire was a lot louder than those that preceded it. It almost seemed to rip the air apart. Norm realized he was now dealing with some kind of crew served, heavy machinegun. He looked at the pistols in his hands and realized, "I think I'm a little under-dressed here."

The only good news, if you could call it that, was the fire was extremely accurate for such a weapon. It had practically chewed up the crates and pallets that Norm had taken cover behind. Despite this, there was not even a single bullet hole in the truck though. That meant he had to find some more cover, but, "Shannon! Stay put! You'll be safe in there."

Shannon yelled back, "Sit and spin, Norm! We're sitting on a fucking bomb, you jack ass!"

Now, Norm knew exactly why they were being so careful about shooting the van. He decided to use it to his advantage and crawled back to the other side. They held their fire when he raised up and yelled back to Shannon, "We? Is Sally in there with you?"

"Yeah? I think this is her?"

What the hell did she mean by that? Norm decided to concentrate on the problem at hand. He moved to the back of the truck and took a quick peek around it, trying to get a good look at the rolldown door. The machinegun cranked back up, but very conservatively. Norm managed to even get off a couple of shots of return fire before ducking back behind his cover. Then he moved back to his original position and told Shannon, "What's the bomb look like?"

"Shit!" was all that Shannon replied. Then after he repeated himself the teenager yelled back, "Give me a minute, ok?"

"Darling, we ain't got a minute," Norm yelled back.

"Look, Norm," Shannon shouted back, "this isn't easy! I'm a little tied up at the moment!"

"You tell me as soon as you get to it," Norm responded when he realized something else was wrong. Why was it that something else was always wrong? He realized that the bad guys had him pinned down, and seemingly they had yet to make a move. Another quick peek, that drew even more near misses from the machinegun, confirmed what Norm had already suspected.

"Norm!" His name was followed by a few more beats on the side of the truck. When Norm let her know he was still there she told him what she found, "It's round, kind of like a drink can. It's got this lit ring around the top and it's getting shorter!"

Norm grumbled. That sounded about like any military charge you could care to name. He yelled back, "Any writing on it?"

"Yeah," she called out, "hang on." A few more seconds of silence went by and Norm suspected they were seconds that none of them had. Then Shannon called back, "ICO-Fifty-Two!"

Now Norm knew exactly why the bad guys were keeping their distance. The ICO stood for Incendiary Compound Ordinance and the number was the charge size. The charge itself was not that big, but it did not have to be. If you put that kind of explosive with enough fuel it could make a fire hot enough to melt this entire building in a few short minutes. That made Norm wonder, so he asked Shannon, "Baby, is there anything else in there with you?"

"Yeah," Shannon replied, "I didn't, like, want to mention this right now, but um, we're sitting on a few million dollars' worth of cocaine. I'm guessing it's the designer stuff from the looks of it."

"How the hell do you know…" Norman forgot about that and gulped. The designer stuff wasn't even really cocaine. It was a mixture of all kinds of fancy chemicals that were, on the whole, highly flammable. A truck this size could provide plenty enough fuel to bring down the entire building and probably then some.

When Norm failed to respond, Shannon did it for him by asking, "That's not good, is it?" When Norm failed to respond again Shannon lashed out with a very command voice, "Get your ass in here and untie us, NOW MISTER!"

"Shannon," Norm responded with as much calm as he could muster. He told himself he was doing it for the kid. He lied to himself about the fact that he even needed to lie to himself right now. He also wished like hell he had dreamed up another plan before rushing in here. Maybe this was a stupid idea? Of course, at the same time, both Sally and Shannon might be dead right now if he had waited.

Sure! Norm figured it out. If they lived, then he'd lie to everybody and tell them it was just all a part of the plan! If they died, well, it really wasn't going to matter, now was it?

"NORM!" Shannon yelled back at him and made him realize that he'd slipped out of reality.

"Look, baby," Norm told her. "You're going to have to disarm this bomb. That door's locked and we got bad guys out here."

Whatever the teenager said next was not very audible and did not completely penetrate the walls of the truck. Norm stuck his ear to the wall, and he was pretty sure he heard wrong. Shannon did not use that kind of language, or that was going to be Norm's story anyway. Finally, she yelled at him, "I'm in high school! I take shop! Not bomb disposal!"

One more time, Norm went and tried both directions of the truck. Each time the machinegun sounded off and cut some fair-sized holes in the sheet metal wall of the building. He took a good look at the holes and then he said to himself, "I think Shannon's right. We might be fucked."

When he went back to his space where he could hear her, it was obvious the little girl had heard him do it. Now the tone in her voice had completely changed. This time it was very obvious she was crying, "Please don't leave me again!"

"Damn," Norm mumbled, "why did she have to go and do that?"

Chapter 24

The only thing that Jake had said when they passed out the heavy weapons from the trunk of Garcia's car was, "I thought I told you to bring the good stuff!"

It was Bob Johnson, as he slipped into his body armor, who laughed and replied, "This is the good stuff." To illustrate his point, he picked up a shotgun and racked it. Then Garcia shook his head in resignation and handed him a box of shells so he could really load the weapon. Johnson took them and shrugged, "Oh, yeah. Might need these! Right! Good call!"

Jake tried telling himself that there was very little chance that they would wind up in a real fight anyway. This was not the army. This was not a war zone. His guys had followed a fashion model here after all. With that being the case, what was it they were likely to find at this place? A shipment of stolen beauty supplies?

The sound of a full-scale battle erupted just behind the trees. It started with something that sounded like an artillery barrage and then, after a small war, it sounded like somebody was using a great big cannon, really fast. Jake mumbled to himself, "That's one heavy duty hair dryer in there."

Cal understood what Jake had just said and developed a very strange look. He then shook it off and decided he did not want to know.

At this point Johnson looked at their trunk of assorted shotguns, rifles, and a few really small machineguns and said, "Um, we might need some more guns here."

Jake took a hunting rifle and let Amy and Tony have the two submachine-pistols that he estimated were probably worthless for hitting anything at a distance. He figured they probably couldn't hit any targets anyway so what could it hurt to let them spray and pray? He pointed to them, "Base of fire."

Tony nodded in the affirmative and then Amy asked the question on everyone's mind, "Gotya, boss. Now, um, what's that mean?"

At that time, Jake made the command decision that all of his command decisions, from this point forward, were probably worthless. He closed the trunk of the car and told all of them, "Follow me in a line." He kept his commands simple, "I'll be in front, and Hiller you'll be in the rear. You do know where the rear is, right?" She nodded that she did, so Jake asked, "Everybody ready?"

They all checked over their gear and began nodding. Jake could not fault them for a lack of enthusiasm, at least. He hoped it would not get them something like, say, dead. With that cheery thought in mind, Jake nodded for them to follow and suddenly Garcia Alvarez broke out with, "Wait, wait, wait!"

When all eyes went to Garcia, he slapped Johnson on the arm, "Did you remember to lock the car door this time?" Johnson just slapped himself on the forehead like, "Silly me," and then went and did just that. When he got back in line, he nodded to everybody else that he was ready, so Jake led them all into the abyss.

They reached the only open roller door of the warehouse loading docks, and found out what was making that 'big cannon' sound. Jake took cover behind the concrete drop off of the dock. Almost everyone else followed suit and, unfortunately, it was just an almost. Tony rolled out of line and ran for the stairs next to Jake. He was obviously going for the door into the warehouse. Jake reached out with one arm and snatched him over the railing and back down to the parking lot. The metal door turned into Swiss cheese shortly thereafter.

When Tony saw the ripped-up door he gulped and then angrily stated, "That's no fair! Man, that's a steel door!"

"And that's a seventy-five caliber in there, genius," Jake told him with even more hostility than earlier. He then looked back at his line of people, all properly scared, and began to tell them to lay down suppression fire. He checked himself and changed his order with, "Stay here and keep that machinegun busy."

Calvin raised his hand and asked, "Preferably by some other means than letting them shoot holes in us, right?"

Jake could not believe he was fielding this question. He just agreed with the man by saying, "That would not be my first choice, no." When none of them got it he told them, "Shoot back!" Amy slapped herself on the forehead and said, "Duh! Why didn't we think of that?" She gave the man an eat shit look, but it was too late, he had already taken off.

All eyes went to Calvin and he said, "I think…"

They waited, and waited, and then waited a little longer before Calvin finally said, "He's got a good idea. Let's do what the man says!"

After a few nods of agreement, they all raised up and opened fire over the top of the loading dock. Less than a moment later, after the return fire, they were all back behind cover and Garcia said what was on all their minds as he picked concrete plaster out of his hair, "That always looked so much easier in the movies."

Amy snapped at them. She figured she was probably as scared as anybody else, but she realized she should not be cowering like this. After all, she'd already been in a gun fight today! She knew she could handle herself! Besides that, Shannon was in there and that poor little girl was probably in need of rescue! Coincidentally, Amy also realized she'd rather face the bullets of a giant murderous auto cannon than Barbara any day of the week.

"What are we doing here, people?" Amy growled at them. "Shannon needs us!" They all looked guilty and scared. "Our new boss needs us, too," she told them. That got mixed reviews at best and even Amy realized she was grasping there. Garcia even made a half and half kind of gesture before shrugging that one off.

So, Amy had to play the real card, "Anybody want to tell Barbara what happened here?" That got them up and moving. They rose up with weapons at the ready, screaming like mad men. Those war cries quickly turned to screams of terror when they realized the enemy had a new weapon. He was driving a truck right at the loading dock door that they were hiding behind. Amy yelled out the only sensible military command that she knew, "DUCK!"

The truck flew right over them and everyone was quite thankful that its roaring engine covered the sounds of their screams. After it hit the pavement and ground to a painful sounding halt, probably from its transmission being smashed, they all pretended like they were still making war cries. Johnson even sprang into action, jumped to his feet and tried shooting at the truck with his shotgun. He was still looking at his weapon wondering why it would not fire when Garcia walked up behind him, flipped off the safety, and with a very scornful tone he asked, "You've had that on the whole time, haven't you?"

Johnson was quite adamant when told his partner, "Yeah, well, remember when I almost shot my foot at the range? Safety first!"

Calvin quickly joined them and was frantically calling out and pointing at the truck, "Hold your fire! That's Norm."

Garcia just flippantly replied while still looking at Bob, "Don't worry, man. I don't think there's much danger of us not holding fire. Safety first, right dude?"

Inside the warehouse, Jake was having a hard time of it. He managed the easy part about like he would expect. The fire from the heavy machinegun was enough noise to cover his movements. If there was any problem with that at all, it was the fact that the machinegun was not firing enough! From the sounds of it, neither were his own people and Jake just kind of figured that might be for the best.

Then something happened and he smiled when he realized what it was. The white truck, on the other side of the warehouse, drove off and whoever did that needed a medal. The machinegun guys wasted no time grabbing their assorted gear, abandoning their position, their weapons, and then retreating for all they were worth. Jake saw his chance and he took it.

He did not actually need to kill all of these guys, and in fact, he needed one alive. He picked the last straggler, stepped out from behind a shipping crate, and put the butt of his rifle right in the guy's eyes. It was more like the man ran into the weapon than Jake had to swing it. It was good enough because the guy wound up on the floor. By the time the man could see again, Jake already had the other end of the weapon pointed at the same spot he had aimed his butt stock.

The man, still lying on the floor, looked terrified. He slowly raised his hands. Then his head exploded, and the floor was smeared with what used to be the guy's brains and blood. Jake quickly swung around and looked for the source of the shot that he had not even heard. He quickly spotted another man in a white jumpsuit. The guy was standing a long way off at the back door of the warehouse. He also had a rifle and was already pointing it at Jake. Now the score was a little more even with Jake's weapon pointed at him.

Jake did not fire. The range was a decent distance, but still an easy shot with this weapon. What Jake realized was that the same was obviously true for the other guy. There was also the little problem of why this guy had shot his own man instead of Jake. Whatever the answer was, it took off with the guy who did not stick around to see if Jake would shoot back. Jake lowered his weapon when the target was gone. He gritted his teeth and then headed back to his own people. Unfortunately, as he found out, the crisis was not quite over yet.

Chapter 25

The last thing that Shannon remembered seeing before they put the tape over her eyes was that oversized coke can that the white-suited goon had placed in the back of the truck. She would have probably never even known what it was except the guy told her as he taped up her mouth. When Shannon heard them roll down the van door, she tried to make herself think. She told herself that the first thing people did in situations like this was panic. It was of small comfort to know that she was doing it in the right order.

Shannon almost screamed when she heard the large ripping explosion. It took her a moment to realize that she would already be dead if it were the bomb going off. The gunfire that followed suddenly brought her back to reality and gave her some hope.

Unfortunately, that did almost nothing for her unfortunate companion in this mess. Shannon had guessed that the girl was this Sally person. The blond was already tied up when Shannon first got tossed in. The goon squad had not bothered with any introductions and Shannon never had the time to get a good look. These guys had been pretty quick about tying them back to back and then resorting to duct tape! Whoever the girl was, she had never really stopped trying to scream and kick for the entire time.

Shannon finally worked the tape off her mouth because she wanted to tell the woman, "Will you stop that already!" The ropes were bad enough without this girl making them rub against the skin! It was at that point when Norm showed up and Shannon got his attention. She had not really expected it to be Norm, but on reflection, that was less of a surprise than Amy and Tony figuring out their next step. Shannon felt kind of guilty about doubting them when Norm told her that the new round of shooting was everybody else showing up. She had little time to worry about it though. Just after that, Norm told her to, "Hang on!" and that this new round of shooting was a good diversion and, 'their chance.'

Shannon had no idea what he was talking about, but the one thing she was certain of was, there was no way she could hang on to anything. Her hands were behind her back and now she was laying on her side, with Sally still firmly attached to her back, and looking at a ticking bomb with her blindfold off. Then it got worse when she heard the truck cranking up.

Shannon yelled in futility, "NO! NO! NORM! Don't!!!"

Whatever the truck had jumped made Shannon absolutely sure that they had just gone over a cliff. She and Sally went flying and the only good news here was that the pile of cocaine provided for some cushioning when they landed. After that, Shannon was not sure if it was the truck or her that was making the loud moans. All she came to realize, after she got her wind back, was that another light bar had vanished from the ring around the top of the bomb. It was over halfway gone now, and even with only shop class under her belt, Shannon could figure out that she was running out of time.

Outside they were all gathered around the back of the truck, most of them just as spectators. Norm and Tony were trying to get the lock off the door. Jake could not express, in words, exactly how this looked like a monumental waste of time. Then they told him why they were doing it. Norm even told him about the bomb.

Amy complained, "Why don't you just shoot the lock, Norm?"

Jake answered, "That only works in the movies. Was she sure about that ring of lights?"

Norm was grunting as he and Tony worked a pry bar on the door itself, "Why don't you ask her yourself?"

Jake walked over to the side of the truck and banged on it, "Shannon! Is there a little green light around the top of that thing?"

The girl sounded scared, confused, and even a little bit angry, but she replied like a trooper, "No, it's yellow now."

Jake thought about it and then told her, "Ok, kid. Look, that's a standardized M-14, static free, energy release trigger. All you got to do is unscrew the cap to disconnect the battery."

"Um," she said with great fear that quickly turned to anger when she yelled back, "IN ENGLISH!"

Jake grunted again and then he thought some more, "Um, are there any extra wires or stuff that's attached to the bomb?"

"I don't see any wires," she told him back.

"Do you see that little black thing in the middle of the lights?"

It took a second but, she did reply, "Yeah and there's nothing on it."

"All you got to do is unscrew that," Jake told her with some relief.

Then Jake got the bad news, "Yeah, that might be easy enough if I wasn't TIED UP! Do you people get the meaning of that word!?"

Jake grumbled beneath his breath, "Two words! God, what are they teaching these kids today?" He then yelled back, "Get it off, Shannon. That's an order." As an added incentive his afterthought was, "Or I'll tell your Mom!"

"Oh, yeah," Shannon called back out. "Like what's she going to do? Ground me?" The teenager changed her tone again, "I'll do what I can, ok?"

Jake got even tougher, "Not what you can! You do it, kid!" Jake walked back to the door and then told everyone else, "All right, all of you not working on the door, clear out!"

No one moved. Jake repeated his command. This time he did it very harshly, but still no one moved. That was all except for Amy who angrily stomped up to the back of the truck and pushed Tony and Norm to the side. When she pulled out her pistol and stuck it on the lock, everyone else ran for cover. Amy gulped, squinted, and then pulled the trigger. She still had her eyes closed when Jake walked up to her and carefully took the gun out of her hand. He then looked down at the lock and said, "I'll be damned. It actually worked."

When they rolled-up the door, they found Shannon and Sally in the middle of the truck. They were laying on their sides on what had to be the most expensive bed that Jake had ever seen. There were thousands, if not tens of thousands, of little baggies of white stuff. Jake needed no lab test to tell him what that was. What he did need was someone to tell him why anyone would want to blow all of it up. Of course, that would not happen now. The main reason for that was Shannon. She spit the bomb's little flat disk of a battery out of her mouth and then scornfully accused her rescuers, "Well, it took you guys long enough!"

Garcia stuck his head in the van as Norm and Amy freed the captives. His eyes got big and he said, "Holy shit! I can retire!"

Tony slapped him on the head, "Stop joking around, man. What we got here is the biggest bust we ever made. I'm going to be getting interviewed by Jessie Walsh now, buddy!"

Amy led Shannon out of the van, hovering over her like a worried mother hen. The teen was not very receptive to that, or to Tony either. She told him as she got out of the truck, "Oh, yeah, and thanks, I'm fine, too!"

He snapped back, "I told you to stay in the car."

She motioned to the back of the truck, "Where do you think I've been the whole time? Moron!"

It was Johnson who was the only one who sounded panicked. He was looking out towards the property gates where they had parked their vehicles. He suddenly realized, "Hey, guys! I think somebody stole my car!"

Jake looked in that direction, but he quickly forgot about the car as he watched a horde of armored personnel carriers come crashing on the property at full speed. He kept right on watching as they took up a standard formation for unloading infantry. It was exactly what the vehicles did, and even Jake had to admit that the soldiers of the Three Hundred and Twenty-first Panzer Grenadiers came at them as professionally as anybody could.

As the heavily armed troopers stopped in a battle line with their weapons raised, and just short of the truck, it was Amy who gulped and pointed out, "All right, guys. I think they're really going to shoot us this time."

Nobody paid particular heed to Amy's observation, but they all got worried when Norm pointed out, "Unfortunately, I think Amy's right."

Horst came swaggering up, but this time he stayed behind his men. The German colonel's position told Jake that both Amy and Norm were right. Jake looked in the van, he looked at his people, then he looked back to the Germans. He put his weapon on the ground, and as he walked towards the firing squad, he calmly told his people, "Don't worry. I'll handle this."

Chapter 26

The Palace, which is what the main government building was called here, was already a century and a half old. The construction had been started by the original Texan colonists. Then construction was halted for a war that was way back on Earth. When the Republic of Texas found itself bankrupt because of the war and could no longer afford the colony, they sold it to a private company. This real estate transaction had also halted construction on the building. Eventually, work on the Palace had been started back by the company until the colonists revolted and it was halted once again.

In the years following, a host of nations and international conglomerates had run the colony and this building was the living symbol of that. It was a gaudy, over built, miss mash of styles and time periods. The current Governor, Helen Crass, a local who was appointed by the United Nations back on Earth, was spearheading the movement to have most of the building torn down and 'remodeled' in one style that she thought would really symbolize the human presence on this world. Naturally, there were plenty of people who disagreed with her on exactly what that style was.

It all came down to a matter of money and who could raise most of it. That faction would more than likely have the most say in how the Palace was rebuilt. Having an office in the building helped too. For one thing, besides the obvious, it gave the governor a platform to raise more funds than anyone else. That was why she turned even the most mundane function into an event and put her hand out every single time.

The governor was doing just that right now. The US Council was present with several members of his staff and Helen had always calculated they were good for a lump sum every time they walked in the door. They got invited to a lot of parties. Since they could not afford to be showed up by the officials of other nations, the Americans never had any choice but to attend.

Other than the money, Helen was most curious about one particular detail that the Americans seemed to have overlooked, "Well this party is for your new man, Barton. Why is he not here?"

It was that annoying little man with the buzz cut, Gary Moss, who answered for his boss, "Well, he is currently indisposed your excellency. I'm afraid that we still have him being debriefed by our legal team. It's uh…" Moss cleared his throat, "some treaty matters."

Whitman, his boss, smiled politely and said, "I'm sure we can hand over his credentials in a more private setting."

Helen graciously smiled even if she knew they were full of shit. In fact, she never would have asked the question had she not already known why. If there was one thing she loved, even more than taking American money, it was putting their ambassador on the spot. She saw yet another chance to do so when her eye caught sight of a certain individual entering the room. She had only ever seen his photograph, but he was recognizable enough. That was made doubly so by the black man who was following him. Helen had met that man, Norman Scoggins, on multiple occasions. She had heard even more about him on the side.

Jake Barton was dressed for the occasion and his tag along companion had at least put on a coat. That was something of a miracle, even if it looked like he had bought it at a thrift store. Barton marched right up to the governor and shook hands, then he nodded to the American diplomats, and finally addressed the other man in the little crowd. "Chief Summers. Good to see you again. We keep running into each other today."

Summers was stewing. His face was turning red, but he kept his mouth shut. He did manage to point a finger at Norm. The governor pushed his finger back down and quietly told him, "Not here."

Moss cleared his throat again, "Um, Major." He forced a smile, "Jake. I thought that…"

"No," Jake cut him off with, "plans changed." He retrieved some neatly folded papers from the inside of his coat and handed them over to Helen, "I think you need these, Your Excellency."

Helen took them and quickly passed them off to one of her staffers, "You couldn't wait to the official presentation, Major? I think I would love for you to stick around and tell us about your extraordinary day. From what I've been hearing, they put you to work rather quickly."

"Oh no, ma'am," Jake told her with a smile. He then looked around the room at all the lavishly dressed people and said, "I think this will do. I don't have any money, oh except one hundred marks, which I will gladly donate to your rebuilding fund. The chief here can pay you."

Summers did bust out with, "That man, Scoggins, I will…"

"That man, Chief," Jake told him, "was working undercover on my orders. As it so happens, he, in cooperation with Herr Oberst Horst and the Three Twenty

First Intel team, managed to stop a major drug shipment from reaching the streets."

Of course, what Jake was not going to say was that the drugs had most likely been stolen from the Germans in the first place. Unless Jake missed his guess, that theft had been facilitated by Horst himself until the crew in the white jumpsuits had double crossed him. Jake was not sure of the specifics but that was about the only thing that made sense so far. Now the drugs were safely back in the German property room where no doubt Horst was busy arranging another theft with people that he could trust a little better.

Summers replied to that, "He's not wanted for drug smuggling."

"Oh, yes," Jake kept right on smiling and he even laughed. He got the Governor to do that as well. Then Jake said, "I couldn't tell you at the time, but Roy Kingsley was Agent Scoggins confidential informant on the matter. When the smugglers found out, they killed Kingsley and tried to frame Agent Scoggins for it. We know this because our witness, a Miss Sally..?" Jake had to look to Norm.

Norm just shrugged, "Don't look at me. I can't pronounce her name either."

"Yeah, well," Jake went on, "they tried to blow up Sally with the same kind of device that they killed Roy with. The German ordinance specialists can testify to that much." Jake gave a sly look at Whitman and Moss, "As it turns out it was a stolen US military ordinance."

Whitman coughed. It was Moss that stated, "Yeah, I think we have some paperwork on that."

The governor nodded to Jake and asked, "And did you catch these drug smugglers?"

"Well, not us," Jake told her. "The Wehrmacht tracked down a local plastic surgeon, and as it turned out, he and Mrs. Kingsley, the wife of the Confidential Informant, were involved. Unfortunately, they resisted arrest and the Wehrmacht got control of the situation with typical German efficiency."

Whitman coughed again and this time almost spit out his drink "They killed them?"

The Governor remained calm when she asked Jake, "You do realize she was one of our top models? Mrs. Kingsley that is?"

What could Jake say to that? He really did not care. He had to hand over the bodies to Horst in order to really seal the deal. Even his threat to blow up the drugs was not enough to deter Horst. The guy figured he could take them before Jake could get the chance and he was probably right. It was Jake pointing out that if he caught Roy's murderers, the Texans would owe him a favor. As it turned out, Horst was quite pleased with that offer. The only hitch was he needed Sally and the Rangers alive to make that work.

Jake bowed to the governor, "If you will excuse me, Your Excellency, I do look forward to receiving my badge and ID card at your leisure." He then nodded to Norm and prepared to leave. He did stop for one parting comment, and that was directed to Chief Summers, "One hundred marks."

The Governor already had her hand out.

When they reached the station and parked their car, Norm got out and walked over to a good spot where he could see the beach and the sea. He put his hands in his pockets and just watched the little caps of glowing greenish foam in a sea of darkness. He did not see Jake walk up but he heard him. He told the man, "You got balls of steel, you know that?"

Jake stopped next to the man and wondered if that were an insult or compliment. He decided he really did not want to know so he changed the subject, "And you could have at least worn a tie."

"You're lucky I even tucked my shirt in," Norm replied. They both stood in silence for a minute and then finally Norm worked up enough nerve to break it, "You do realize this ain't over yet."

Jake stayed vague, "Why whatever do you mean, Agent Scoggins?"

Norm almost laughed but then he said, "You and me both damn well know that whatever they used to blow up ole Roy Boy wasn't the same thing as that bomb little Shannon tried to eat."

Jake knew one or two other things, but for the time being he decided that he would keep those to himself. He wondered if Norm had figured all of that other stuff out too. It was probably a safe bet so what was the point in dredging it all up? Jake remained silent.

Norm filled that silence with, "Well, my war is over today. That is all except for trying to explain this to my wife. You," he looked right at Jake and poked him in the chest of the expensive suit, "have a bigger war to go fight right now."

"Yeah," Jake was all ears, "and what might that be?"

"When we was coming down the drive," Norm told him, "I noticed that the other chopper was back up at the hanger." He looked over his shoulder towards the station and saw the silhouette of a loan individual in the window. He then looked back to Jake, "I think I'd rather deal with my wife right now, so good luck, Jake."

As Norm started to walk to his car he did turn and leave a passing thought, "Just remember that we have a saying down here in the Arch. You're a military man so I'm sure you're familiar with anagrams. Just always remember T-N-O."

Jake looked up at the window and saw the person in the window. He could guess who it was. He then looked back to Norm and asked, "Yeah? And what's that mean, Agent Scoggins?"

The man did not bother looking back as he vanished into the dark, "Trust No One."

Jake thought about that for a minute. Then he decided that was for tomorrow. He went back to the room where they had stashed all of his stuff. It looked like he would really be staying here, at least for the night. With everything that had happened today, the last thing on Jake's mind had been finding a hotel room. After Johnson had his car stolen in the middle of a shootout, Jake had also questioned the wisdom of getting a room at all.

Jake changed clothes into a T-shirt and pair of shorts. He also decided that flip-flops would do for footwear. This was going to be a different kind of meeting than the one he had with the governor. He stopped by the commissary, said hi to Cal, and grabbed a beer from the fridge. Then he headed up the stairs to Operations. What he saw there, kind of surprised him.

Barbara Reilly did not look anything like what he had expected. She was a lean woman, with shoulder length brown hair, dressed in slacks and a red turtleneck. She was drinking a cup of coffee in what had to be her favorite mug, and above all else she had an air of being relaxed. On top of all that, Jake had to admit that she had a very nice ass on her.

As Jake stood there on the stairs and looked at her, Barbara turned and with an air of humor asked him, "Not what you were expecting?"

Jake finished his climb up the stairs, and she offered him coffee, but he pointed to his beer. He leaned up against one of the cluttered counters and told her, "To be honest. No, you aren't."

She smiled and even giggled, "Well I left my green skin and broomstick at the other station." Then she added, "Now it's my turn."

Jake shrugged, "Not what you were expecting either?"

Barbara struck a thoughtful pose and said, "I think this is the part where I'm supposed to say, 'Aren't you a little short for a storm trooper?'"

Jake laughed along with her and said, "Well I'm glad we got all that out of the way. Now we can get down to the part where you tell me you resent me even being here."

Barbara was a little more serious, but she kept it light, "They told me you were very perceptive. That's good, Mr. Barton, I like that. They also told me you had a very busy day."

"Yeah," again Jake shrugged. "Well it did not turn out exactly the way I would have wanted, still we managed to take down the bad guys anyway, I think. It's just not exactly how we did it back on Earth."

"Yeah," Barbara nodded in agreement and was very serious, "Welcome to my world, Mr. Barton. These are good kids we have here. We do the best we can do with almost no budget at all. I barely have enough money to keep those choppers and our boats operational. Oh hey, let's not even think about giving my people a raise every now and then."

Jake snickered, "So you don't like the governor either."

"Helen Crass isn't the problem here, Mr. Barton," Barbara told him.

Jake took a sip of beer and pointed to himself, "No, it's guys like me."

Barbara took a moment before replying. She was serious but not hostile when she did, "Ok, if you want to go there. Yeah, guys like you. The last two guys they sent out here to hold your job, well the first one wound up blowing his brains out and the other one, seventy two hours, and then he marched right back over to the US Consul and filed his retirement papers."

Jake laughed and then commented, "Good thing to know I'm already a third of the way to retirement."

Now Barbara did sound a bit hostile, "I don't think it's funny, Mr. Barton. You know that last big war they had. We never saw any of it here unless it was on the news. Despite that, we sent our friends, our family, off to go fight in it. They were people like my dad, my brother, my husband, and none of them came home."

Barbara then turned away from him before she went on. "Then one day a starship jumps into orbit and tells us everything will be all right. We're going to let everybody else run your lives for you. People like my father and brother, everything they had bled for was just erased. Do you know that both of them served at this very station? My father, well," she took a minute to compose herself, "he ran this place for twenty-six years. His father another twenty before that. Even my husband, Shannon's father, he worked here."

Jake became a bit more somber, "And I'm walking on their graves?"

If Barbara even heard the question, she did not show it, "My daughter Shannon, you know the one you almost blew up today? This place is all she has ever known. This isn't a profession, Mr. Barton. This isn't just some duty station. This is our home. This is our family."

"Well, first off," Jake rose from his seat, "I wasn't the one that took her joy riding on a criminal investigation."

"I know," Barbara replied resolutely, "and I'll deal with Tony and Amy when the time is right."

"You know, lady," Jake told her as they squared off, "if you want to point fingers about who almost got your daughter killed…"

"This isn't about pointing fingers, Mr. Barton," Barbara told him. "And when you've been the boss for longer than a day then, maybe, you'll understand that."

It was Jake's turn to ignore the statement and continue his thought, "maybe Agent Reilly, you should start by taking a real good look at yourself."

She took a step back and her face turned red. Barbara then blurted out, "And exactly what is that supposed to mean?"

"It means, Barb," Jake told her, "that if your kids, and that includes your biological one too, had been more important to you than snubbing me, then just maybe none of this would have ever happened."

"You're out of line," Barbara bit back.

"No," Jake told her, "I'm making a point. These aren't bad kids you got here, Barbara. They got guts and that is a start. What they are sorely lacking in is leadership."

"Oh," Barbara snarled and turned it on him. "And I suppose you're the one to give it to them?"

He surprised her in return by saying, "Well somebody better start. This is your world, Barbara. I don't need to tell you how dangerous it is out there. Unless these kids get proper training and guidance, and to hell with the damn budget, one of them, if not all of them, are going to get killed. Just like your Agent Nguyen almost managed to this morning."

"I'll have you know," she came back with.

Jake cut her off, "If you had been here you might have stopped Nguyen from running off in the middle of her shift. If you had been here, then Norm might not have gone off halfcocked. If you had been here, then your daughter might not have wound up tied to a bomb." She almost said something, but Jake cut her off once more, "Tell me I'm wrong."

Now Barbara surprised Jake, yet again. She relaxed. She smiled and then she reached out for a shake with crossed arms. She was quite calm when she told him, "Maybe you'll live after all, Mr. Barton. You certainly have to watch that temper of yours, though."

Jake shook her hand, looked her in the eye and she did not blink. He finally nodded good night and began his walk back down the stairs. As he did, he heard her say, "Oh and by the way, Mr. Barton, I think you have a cute ass too."

Jake just kept on walking.

TO BE CONTINUNED

Made in the USA
Monee, IL
19 June 2024

60155981R00073